Lincolnshire
COUNTY COUNCIL

COMMUNITIES, CULTURAL SERVICES
and ADULT EDUCATION
**This book should be returned on or before
the last date shown below.**

NC 1

To renew or order library
or visit v
You will require a
Ask any

010

D1492368

EC. 199 (LIBS): RS/L5/19

04507704

THE SANTANGELI
MARRIAGE

THE SANTANGELI MARRIAGE

BY

SARA CRAVEN

MILLS & BOON

Pure reading pleasure™

First published in Great Britain 2008
Large Print edition 2009
Harlequin Mills & Boon Limited,
Eton House, 18-24 Paradise Road,
Richmond, Surrey TW9 1SR

ISBN: 978 0 263 20587 9

Set in Times Roman 15 on 16½ pt.
16-0509-64460

Printed and bound in Great Britain
by CPI Antony Rowe, Chippenham, Wiltshire

CHAPTER ONE

THE glass doors of the Clinica San Francesco whispered open, and every head turned to observe the man who came striding out of the darkness into the reception area.

If Lorenzo Santangeli was aware of their scrutiny, or if he sensed that there were far more people hanging around than could be deemed strictly necessary at that time of night, and most of them female, he gave no sign.

His lean, six-foot-tall body was clad in the elegance of evening clothes, and his ruffled shirt was open at the throat, his black tie thrust negligently into the pocket of his dinner jacket.

One of the loitering nurses, staring at his dishevelled dark hair, murmured to her colleague with unknowing accuracy that he looked as if he'd just rolled out of bed, and the other girl sighed wistfully in agreement.

He was not classically handsome, but his thin face, with its high cheekbones, heavy-lidded golden-brown eyes and that mobile, faintly sensual mouth, which looked as if it could curl in a sneer and smile in heart-stopping allure with equal ease, had a dynamism that went beyond mere attractiveness. And every woman looking at him felt it like a tug to the senses.

The fact that he was frowning, and his lips were set in a grim line, did nothing to reduce the force of his blatantly masculine appeal.

He looked, it was felt, just as a loving son should when called unexpectedly to the bedside of a sick father.

Then, as the clinic's director, Signor Martelli, emerged from his office to greet him, the crowd, hurriedly realising it should be elsewhere, began to fade swiftly and unobtrusively away.

Renzo wasted no time on niceties. He said, his voice sharp with anxiety, 'My father—how is he?'

'Resting comfortably,' the older man responded. 'Fortunately an ambulance was summoned immediately when it happened, so there was no delay in providing the appropriate treatment.' He smiled reassuringly. 'It was not a serious attack, and we expect the Marchese to make a complete recovery.'

Renzo expelled a sigh of relief. 'May I see him?'

'Of course. I will take you to him.' Signor Martelli pressed a button to summon a lift to the upper floors. He gave his companion a sidelong glance. 'It is, of course, important that your father avoids stress, and I am told that he has been fretting a little while awaiting your arrival. I am glad that you are here now to set his mind at rest.'

'It is a relief to me also, *signore*.' The tone was

courteous, but it had a distancing effect. So far, it seemed to warn, and no further.

The clinic director had heard that Signor Lorenzo could be formidable, and this was all the confirmation he needed, he thought, relapsing into discreet silence.

Renzo had been expecting to find his father's private room peopled by consultants and quietly shod attendants, with Guillermo Santangeli under sedation and hooked up to monitors and drips.

But instead his father was alone, propped up by pillows, wearing his own striking maroon silk pyjamas and placidly turning over the pages of a magazine on international finance. Taking the place of machinery was a large and fragrant floral arrangement on a side table.

As Renzo checked, astonished, in the doorway, Guillermo peered at him over his glasses. 'Ah,' he said. *'Finalmente.'* He paused. 'You were not easy to trace, my son.'

Fretting, Renzo thought, might be an exaggeration, but the slight edge to his words was unmistakable. He came forward slowly, his smile combining ruefulness and charm in equal measure. 'Nevertheless, Papa, I am here now. And so, thankfully, are you. I was told you had collapsed with a heart attack.'

'It was what they call "an incident".' Guillermo shrugged. 'Alarming at the time, but soon dealt with. I am to rest here for a couple of days, and then I will be allowed to return home.' He sighed. 'But I have to take medication, and cigars and brandy have been forbidden—for a while at least.'

'Well, the cigars, at any rate, must be counted as a blessing,' Renzo said teasingly as he took his father's hand and kissed it lightly.

His father pulled a face. 'That is also Ottavia's opinion. She has just left. I have her to thank for the pyjamas and the flowers, also for summoning help so promptly. We had just finished dinner when I became ill.'

Renzo's brows lifted. 'Then I am grateful to her.' He pulled up a chair and paused. 'I hope Signora Alesconi did not go on my account.'

'She is a woman of supreme tact,' said his father. 'And she knew we would wish to talk privately. There is no other reason. I have assured her that you no longer regard our relationship as a betrayal of your mother's memory.'

Renzo's smiled twisted a little. '*Grazie*. You were right to say so.' He hesitated. 'So may I now expect to have a new stepmother? If you wished to—formalise the situation I—I would welcome…'

Guillermo lifted a hand. 'There is no question of that. We have fully discussed the matter, but decided that we both value our independence too highly and remain content as we are.' He removed his glasses and put them carefully on the locker beside his bed. 'And while we are on the subject of marriage, where is your wife?'

Well, I walked headlong into that, thought Renzo, cursing under his breath. Aloud, he said, 'She is in England, Papa—as I think you know.'

'Ah, yes.' His father gave a meditative nod. 'Where she went shortly after your honeymoon, I believe, and has remained ever since.'

Renzo's mouth tightened. 'I felt—a period of adjustment might be helpful.'

'A curious decision, perhaps,' said Guillermo. 'Considering the pressing reasons for your marriage. You are the last of the line, my dear Lorenzo, and as you approached the age of thirty, without the least sign of abandoning your bachelor life and settling down, it became imperative to remind you that you had a duty to produce a legitimate heir to carry on the Santangeli name—both privately and professionally.'

He paused. 'You seemed to accept that. And with no other candidate in mind, you also consented to marry the girl your late mother always intended for you—her beloved goddaughter Marisa Brendon. I wish to be sure that advancing age has not damaged my remembrance, and that I have the details of this agreement correct, you understand?' he added blandly.

'Yes.' Renzo set his teeth. *Advancing age?* he thought wryly. *How long did crocodiles survive?* 'You are, of course, quite right.'

'Yet eight months have passed, and still you have no good news to tell me. This would have been a disappointment in any circumstances, but in view of the evening's events my need to hear that the next generation is established becomes even more pressing. From now on I must take more care, they tell me. Moderate my lifestyle. In other words, I have been made aware of my own mortality. And I confess that I would dearly like to hold my first grandchild in my arms before I die.'

Renzo moved restively, 'Papa—you will live for many years yet. We both know that.'

'I can hope,' said Guillermo briskly. 'But that is not the point.' He leaned back against his pillows, adding quietly, 'Your bride can hardly give you an heir, *figlio mio*, if you do not share a roof with her, let alone a bed. Or do you visit her in London, perhaps, in order to fulfil your marital obligations?'

Renzo rose from his chair and walked over to the window, lifting the slats of the blind to look out into the darkness. An image of a girl's white face rose in his mind, her eyes blank and tearless, and a feeling that was almost shame twisted like a knife in his guts.

'No,' he said at last. 'I do not.'

'Then why not?' his father demanded. 'What can be the problem? Yes, the marriage was arranged for you, but so was my own, and your mother and I soon came to love each other deeply. And here you have been given a girl, young, charming, and indisputably innocent. Someone, moreover, you have known for much of your life. If she was not to your taste you should have said so.'

Renzo turned and gave him an ironic look. 'It does not occur to you, Papa, that maybe the shoe is on the other foot and Marisa does not want me?'

'*Che sciocchezze!*' Guillermo said roundly. 'What nonsense. When she stayed with us as a child it was clear to everyone that she adored you.'

'Unfortunately, now she is older, her feelings are very different,' Renzo said dryly. 'Particularly where the realities of marriage are concerned.'

Guillermo pursed his lips in exasperation. 'What can you be saying? That a man of your experience with women cannot seduce his own wife? You should have made duty a pleasure, my son, and used your honeymoon to make her fall in love with you all over again.' He paused. 'After all, she was not forced to marry you.'

Renzo gave his father a level look. 'I think we both know that is not true. Once she'd discovered from that witch of a cousin how deeply she was indebted to our family she had little choice in the matter.'

Guillermo frowned heavily. 'You did not tell her— explain that it was the dying wish of your mother, her *madrina*, that financial provision should continue to be made for her?'

'I tried, but it was useless. She knew that Mama wanted us to marry. For her, it all seemed part of the same ugly transaction.' He paused. 'And the cousin also made her aware that when I proposed to her I had a mistress. After such revelations, the honeymoon was hardly destined to go well.'

'The woman has much to answer for, it seems,' Guillermo said icily. 'But you, my son, were a fool not to have settled matters with the beautiful Lucia long before you approached your marriage.'

'If stupidity were all, I could live with it,' Renzo said with quiet bitterness. 'But I was also unkind. And I cannot forgive myself for that.'

'I see,' his father said slowly. 'Well, that is bad, but it is more important to ask yourself if your wife can be persuaded to forgive you.'

'Who knows?' Renzo's gesture was almost helpless. 'I thought a breathing space—time apart to consider what we had undertaken—would help. And at the beginning I wrote to her regularly—telephoned and left messages. But there was never any reply. And as the weeks passed the hope of any resolution became more distant.' He paused, before adding expressionlessly, 'I told myself, you understand, that I would not beg.'

Guillermo put his fingertips together and studied them intently. 'A divorce, naturally, could not be countenanced,' he said at last. 'But from what you are telling me it seems there might be grounds for annulment?'

'No,' Renzo said harshly, his mouth set. 'Do not be misled. The marriage—exists. And Marisa is my wife. Nothing can change that.'

'So you say,' his father commented grimly. 'But you could be wrong. Your grandmother honoured me with a visit yesterday to inform me that your current liaison with Doria Venucci is now talked of openly.'

'Nonna Teresa.' Renzo bit out the name. 'What a gratifying interest she takes in all the details of my life, especially those she considers less than savoury. And how could a woman with such a mind produce such a gentle, loving daughter as my mother?'

'It has always mystified me too,' Guillermo admitted. 'But for once her gossip-mongering may be justified. Because she believes it can only be a matter of time before someone tells Antonio Venucci exactly how his wife has been amusing herself while he has been in Vienna.'

He saw his son's brows lift, and nodded. 'And that, my dear Lorenzo, could change everything, both for you and for your absent wife. Because the scandal that would follow would ruin any remaining chance of a reconciliation with her—if that is what you want, of course.'

'It is what must happen,' Renzo said quietly. 'I cannot allow the present situation to continue any longer. For one thing, I am running out of excuses to explain her absence. For another, I accept that the purpose of our marriage must be fulfilled without further delay.'

'*Dio mio,*' Guillermo said faintly. 'I hope your approach to your bride will be made in more alluring terms. Or I warn you, my son, you will surely fail.'

Renzo's smile was hard. 'No,' he said. 'Not this time. And that is a promise.'

* * *

However, Renzo was thoughtful as, later, he drove back to his apartment. He owned the top floor of a former *palazzo*, the property of an old and noble family who had never seen the necessity to work for their living until it was too late. But although he enjoyed its grace and elegance, he used it merely as a *pied à terre* in Rome.

Because the home of his heart was the ancient and imposing country house deep in the Tuscan country-side where he had been born, and where he'd expected to begin his married life in the specially converted wing, designed to give them all the space and privacy that newlyweds could ever need.

He remembered showing it to Marisa before the wedding, asking if she had any ideas or requirements of her own that could be incorporated, but she'd said haltingly that it all seemed 'very nice', and refused to be drawn further. And she had certainly not com-mented on the adjoining bedrooms that they would occupy after their marriage, with the communicating door.

And if she'd had reservations about sharing the house with her future father-in-law she hadn't voiced those either. On the contrary, she'd always seemed very fond of Zio Guillermo, as she'd been encouraged to call him.

But then, Renzo thought, frowning, apart from agreeing to be his wife in a small wooden voice she hadn't said too much to him at all. Something he should, of course, have noticed but for his other pre-occupations, he conceded, his mouth tightening.

Besides, he was accustomed to the fact that she did not chatter unnecessarily from the days when she'd been a small, silent child, clearly overwhelmed by her surroundings, and through her years as a skinny, tongue-tied adolescent. A time, he recalled ruefully, when she'd constantly embarrassed him by the hero-worship she'd tried inexpertly to hide.

She hadn't even cried at her own christening in London, which he'd attended as a sullenly reluctant ten-year-old, watching Maria Santangeli looking down, her face transfigured, at the lacy bundle in her arms.

His mother had met Lisa Cornell at the exclusive convent school they had both attended in Rome, and they had formed a bond of friendship that had never wavered across the years and miles that separated them.

But whereas Maria had married as soon as she left school, and become a mother within the year, Lisa had pursued a successful career in magazine journalism before meeting Alec Brendon, a well-known producer of television documentaries.

And when her daughter had been born only Maria would do as godmother to the baby. A role she had been more than happy to fill. The name chosen was naturally 'Marisa', the shortened form of Maria Lisa.

Renzo knew that, much as he had been loved, it had always been a sadness to his parents that no other children had followed him into the waiting nurseries at the Villa Proserpina. And this godchild had taken the place of the longed-for daughter in his mother's heart.

He wasn't sure on which visit to Italy she and Lisa Brendon had begun planning the match between their children. He knew only that, to his adolescent disgust, it seemed to have become all too quickly absorbed into family folklore as an actual possibility.

He'd even derisively christened Marisa *'la cicogna'*—the stork—a mocking reference to her long legs and the little beak of a nose that dominated her small, thin face, until his mother had called him to order with unwonted sternness.

But the fact that Marisa was being seriously considered as his future bride had been brought home to him six years ago, when her parents had been killed in a motorway pile-up.

Because, in a devastating aftermath of the accident, it had been discovered that the Brendons had always lived up to and exceeded their income, and that through some fairly typical oversight Alec had failed to renew his life insurance, leaving his only daughter penniless.

At first Maria had begged for the fourteen-year-old girl to be brought to Italy and raised as a member of their family, but for once the ever-indulgent Guillermo had vetoed her plan. If her scheme to turn Marisa into the next Santangeli bride was to succeed—and there was, of course, no guarantee that this would happen—it would be far better, he'd said, for the girl to continue her education and upbringing in England, at their expense, than for Renzo to become so accustomed to her presence in the household that he might begin to regard her simply as an irritating younger sister.

It was a proposition to which his wife had reluctantly acquiesced. And while Marisa had remained in England Renzo had been able to put the whole ridiculous idea of her as his future wife out of his mind.

In any case, he'd had to concentrate on his career, completing his business degree with honours before joining the renowned and internationally respected Santangeli Bank, where he would ultimately succeed his father as chairman. By a mixture of flair and hard work he had made sure he deserved the top job, and that no one would mutter sourly 'boss's son' when he took over.

He was aware that the junior ranks of staff referred to him as 'Il Magnifico', after his namesake Lorenzo de Medici, but shrugged it off with amusement.

Life had been good. He'd had a testing job which provided exhilaration and interest, also allowing him to travel widely. And with his dynastic obligations remaining no more than a small cloud on his horizon he had enjoyed women, his physical needs deliciously catered to by a series of thoroughly enjoyable affairs which, the ladies involved knew perfectly well, would never end in marriage.

But while he'd learned early in his sexual career to return with infinite skill and generosity the pleasure he received, he'd never committed the fatal error of telling any of his *innamoratas* that he loved her—not even in the wilder realms of passion.

Then, three years ago, he had been shocked out of his complacency by his mother's sudden illness. She'd been found to be suffering from an aggressive and inoperable cancer and had died only six weeks later.

'Renzo, *carissimo mio*.' Her paper-thin hand had rested on his, light as a leaf. 'Promise me that my little Marisa will be your wife.'

And torn by sorrow and disbelief at the first real blow life had struck him, he had given her his word, thereby sealing his fate.

Now, as he walked into his apartment, he heard the phone ringing. He ignored it, knowing only too well who was calling, because the clinic would have used the private mobile number he'd left with them—which Doria Venucci did not have.

He recognised that, if he was to stand any chance of retrieving his marriage, she was a luxury he could no longer afford. However, courtesy demanded that he tell her in person that their relationship was over.

Not that she would protest too much. A secret *amour* was one thing. A vulgar scandal which jeopardised her own marriage would be something else entirely, he told himself cynically.

As he walked across his vast bedroom to the bathroom beyond, shedding his clothes as he went, he allowed himself a brief moment of regret for the lush, golden, insatiable body he'd left in bed only a few hours before and would never enjoy again.

But everything had changed now. And at the same time he knew how totally wrong he'd been to become involved with her in the first place. Especially when he'd had no real excuse for his behaviour apart from another infuriating encounter with Marisa's damnable answering machine.

So she still didn't want to speak to him, he'd thought furiously, slamming down his receiver as a bland, anonymous voice had informed him yet again that she was 'not available'. She was still refusing to give him even the slightest chance to make amends to her.

Well, so be it, he had told himself. He was sick of the self-imposed celibacy he'd been enduring since she left, and if she didn't want him he'd go out and find a woman who did.

It had not been a difficult task because, at a party that same evening, he'd met Doria and invited her to a very proper and public lunch with him the following day. Which had been followed, without delay, by a series of private and exceedingly improper assignations in a suite at a discreet and accordingly expensive hotel.

And if he'd embarked on the affair in a mood of defiance, he could not pretend that the damage to his male pride had not been soothed by the Contessa Venucci's openly expressed hunger for him, he thought wryly.

He stepped into the shower cubicle, switching the water to its fullest extent, letting it pound down on his weary body, needing it to eradicate the edginess and confusion of emotions that were assailing him.

It could not be denied that latterly, outside working hours, he had not enjoyed the easiest of relationships with his father. He had always attributed this to his disapproval of Guillermo's year-long liaison with Ottavia Alesconi, having made it coldly clear from the beginning that he felt it was too soon after his mother's death for the older man to embark on such a connection.

And yet did he really have any right to object to his father's wish to find new happiness? The *signora* was a charming and cultivated woman, a childless widow, still running the successful PR company she had begun with her late husband. Someone, moreover, who was quite content to share Guillermo's leisure, but had no ambitions to become his Marchesa.

His father had always seemed so alive and full of vigour, with never a hint of ill health, so tonight's attack must have been a particularly unpleasant shock to her, he thought sombrely, resolving to call on her in person to thank her for her prompt and potentially life-saving efforts on Guillermo's behalf. By doing so he might also make it clear that any initial resentment of her role in his father's life had long since dissipated.

Besides, he thought ruefully, his own personal life was hardly such a blazing success that he could afford to be critical of anyone else's. And maybe it was really his bitter sense of grievance over being cornered into marriage that had brought about the coldness that had grown up between his father and himself.

But he could not allow any lingering animosity, he told himself as he stepped out of the shower and began to dry himself. He had to put the past behind him, where it belonged. Tonight had indeed been a warning—in a number of ways. It was indeed more than time he abandoned his bachelor lifestyle and applied himself to becoming a husband and, in due course, a father.

If, of course, he could obtain the co-operation of his bride—something he'd signally failed to do so far, he thought, staring broodingly in the mirror as he raked his damp hair back from his face with his fingers.

If he was honest, he could admit that he was a man who'd never had to try too hard with women. It wasn't something he was proud of, but, nevertheless, it remained an indisputable fact. And it remained a terrible irony that his wife was the only one who'd greeted his attempts to woo her with indifference at best and hostility at worst.

He'd become aware that he might have a fight on his hands when he'd paid his first visit to her cousin's house in London, ostensibly to invite Marisa to Tuscany for a party his father was planning to celebrate her nineteenth birthday.

Julia Gratton had received him alone, her hard eyes

travelling over him in an assessment that had managed to be critical and salacious at the same time, he'd thought with distaste.

'So, you've come courting at last, *signore*.' Her laugh was like the yap of a small, unfriendly dog. 'I'd begun to think it would never happen. I sent Marisa up to change,' she added abruptly. 'She'll be down presently. In the meantime, let me offer you some coffee.'

He was glad that she'd told him what was being served in those wide, shallow porcelain cups, because there was no other clue in the thin, tasteless fluid that he forced himself to swallow.

So when the drawing room door opened he was glad to put it aside and get to his feet. Where he paused, motionless, the formal smile freezing on his lips as he saw her.

He could tell by the look of displeasure that flitted across Mrs Gratton's thin face that Marisa had not changed her clothes, as instructed, but he was not, he thought, repining.

She was still shy, looking down at the carpet rather than at him, her long curling lashes brushing her cheeks, but everything else about her was different. Gloriously so. And he allowed the connoisseur in him to enjoy the moment. She was slim now, he realised, instead of gawky, and her face was fuller so that her features no longer seemed too large for its pallor.

Her breasts were not large but, outlined by her thin tee shirt, they were exquisitely shaped. Her waist was a handspan, her hips a gentle curve. And those endless legs—*Santa Madonna*—even encased as they were in tight denim jeans he could imagine how they would feel clasped around him, naked, as she explored under his tuition the pleasures of sex.

Hurriedly he dragged his mind back to the social niceties. Took a step forward, attempting a friendly smile. *'Buongiorno*, Maria Lisa.' He deliberately used the version of her name he'd teased her with in childhood. *'Come stai?'*

She looked back at him then, and for the briefest instant he seemed to see in those long-lashed greygreen eyes such a glint of withering scorn that it stopped him dead. Then, next moment, she was responding quietly and politely to his greeting, even allowing him to take her hand, and he told himself that it must have been his imagination.

Because that was what his ego wanted him to think, he told himself bitterly. That it was an honour for this girl to have been chosen as a Santangeli bride, and if *he* had no objections, especially now that he had seen her again, it must follow that she could have none either.

Prompted sharply by her cousin, she accepted the party invitation, and agreed expressionlessly to his suggestion that he should return the next day to discuss the arrangements.

And although she knew—had obviously been told—that the real reason for his visit was to request her formally to become his wife, she gave no sign of either pleasure or dismay at the prospect.

And that in itself should have warned him, he thought in self-condemnation. Instead he'd attributed her lack of reaction to nervousness at the prospect of marriage.

In the past, his sexual partners had certainly not been chosen for their inexperience, but innocence was an essential quality for the girl who would one day bear the Santangeli heir. He had told himself the least he could do was offer her some reassurance about how their relationship would be conducted in its early days—and nights.

Therefore, he'd resolved to promise her that their honeymoon would be an opportunity for them to become properly reacquainted, even be friends, and that he would be prepared to wait patiently until she felt ready to take him as her husband in any true sense.

And he'd meant every word of it, he thought, re-membering how she'd listened in silence, her head half-turned from him, her creamy skin tinged with colour as he spoke.

All the same, he knew he'd been hoping for some reaction—some slight encouragement for him to take her in his arms and kiss her gently to mark their engagement.

But there'd been nothing, then or later. She'd never signalled in any way that she wanted him to touch her, and by offering forbearance he'd fallen, he realised, annoyed, into a trap of his own making.

Because as time had passed, and their wedding day had approached, he'd found himself as awkward as a boy in her cool, unrevealing company, unable to make even the slightest approach to her—something which had never happened to him before.

But what he had not bargained for was losing his temper. And it was the guilt of that which still haunted him.

He sighed abruptly as he knotted a dry towel round his hips. Well, there was no point in torturing himself afresh over that. He ought to go to bed, he thought, and try to catch some sleep for what little remained of the night. But he knew he was far too restless to relax, and that the time could be used to better effect in planning the coming campaign.

He walked purposefully out of the bathroom, ignoring the invitation of the turned-down bed in the room beyond, and proceeded instead down the hallway to the *salotto*.

It was an impressive room, its size accentuated by the pale walls and a signal lack of clutter. He'd furnished it in light colours too, with deep, lavishly cushioned sofas in cream leather, and occasional tables in muted, ashy shades.

The only apparently discordant note in all this pastel restraint was the massive desk, which he loved because it had once belonged to his grandfather, and which now occupied a whole corner of the room in all its mahogany magnificence.

In banking circles he knew that he was viewed as a moderniser, a man with his sights firmly set on the future, alert to any changes in the market. But anyone seeing that desk, he'd always thought dryly, would have guessed immediately that underlying this was a strong respect for tradition and an awareness of what he owed to the past.

He went straight to the desk, extracted a file from one of its brass-handled drawers and, after pouring himself a generous Scotch, stretched out on one of the sofas and began to glance through the folder's contents. An update had been received the previous day, but he'd not had a chance to read it before, and now seemed an appropriate time.

He took a contemplative mouthful of whisky as his eyes scanned swiftly down the printed sheet, then sat up abruptly with a gasp, nearly choking as his drink went down the wrong way and he found himself in imminent danger of spilling the rest everywhere.

He recovered instantly, eyes watering, then set down the crystal tumbler carefully out of harm's way before, his face thunderous, he re-read the unwelcome information that the private surveillance company engaged for the protection of his absentee wife had provided.

'We must advise you,' it stated, 'that since our last report Signora Santangeli, using her maiden name, has obtained paid employment as a receptionist in a private art gallery in Carstairs Place, apparently taking the place of a young woman on maternity leave. In the past fortnight she has lunched twice in the company of the gallery's owner, Mr Corin Langford. She no longer wears her wedding ring. Photographic evidence can be provided if required.'

Renzo screwed the report into a ball and threw it across the room, cursing long and fluently.

He flung himself off the sofa and began to pace restlessly up and down. He did not need any photographs, he thought savagely. Too many of his own affairs had begun over leisurely lunches, so he knew all about satisfying one appetite while creating another—was totally familiar with the sharing of food and wine, eyes meeting across the table, fingers touching, then entwining.

What he did not—could not—recognise was the mental image of the girl on the other side of the table. Marisa smiling back, talking and laughing, the initial shyness in her eyes dancing into confidence and maybe even into desire.

The way she had never once behaved with him. Nor looked at him—or smiled.

Not, of course, that he was jealous, he hastened to remind himself.

Just—angrier than he'd ever been before. Everything that had happened between them in the past paled into insignificance under this—this insult to his manhood. To his status as her husband.

Well, if his reluctant bride thought she could place

the horns on him, she was much mistaken, he vowed in grim silence. Tomorrow he would go to fetch her home, and once he had her back she would not get away from him again. Because he would make very sure that from then on she would think of no one—want no one—but him. That she would be his completely.

And, he told himself harshly, he would enjoy every minute of it.

CHAPTER TWO

'MARISA? My God, it is you. I can hardly believe it.'

The slender girl who'd been gazing abstractedly into a shop window swung round, her lips parting in astonishment as she recognised the tall, fair-haired young man standing behind her.

She said uncertainly, 'Alan—what are you doing here?'

'That should be my question. Why aren't you sipping cappuccino on the Via Veneto?'

The million-dollar question...

'Well, that can pall after a while,' she said lightly. 'And I began to fancy a cup of English tea instead.'

'Oh,' he said. 'And what does Lorenzo the Magnificent have to say about that?'

The note of bitterness in his voice was not lost on her. She said quickly, 'Alan—don't...'

'No,' he said. 'I know. I'm sorry.' He looked past her to the display of upmarket baby clothes she'd been contemplating and his mouth tightened. 'I gather congratulations must be in order?'

'God, no.' Marisa spoke more forcefully than she'd

intended, and flushed when she saw his surprise. 'I—
I mean not for me. A girl I was at school with, Dinah
Newman, is expecting her first, and I want to buy her
something special.'

'Well, you seem to have come to the right place,'
Alan said, inspecting a couple of the price tickets
with raised brows. 'You need to be the wife of a mil-
lionaire banker to shop here.' He smiled at her. 'She
must be quite a friend.'

'Let's just say that I owe her,' Marisa said quietly.

*I owe her for the fact that she recommended me to
Corin Langford, so that I'm now gainfully employed
instead of totally dependent on Renzo Santangeli.
And for not asking too many awkward questions when
I suddenly turned up in London alone.*

'Do you have to do your buying right now?' Alan
asked. 'I just can't believe I've run into you like this.
I was wondering if we could have lunch together.'

She could hardly tell him that her lunch hour was
coming to an end and it was time she went back to
her desk at the Estrello Gallery. She had already instinctively slid her betrayingly ringless left hand into
the pocket of her jacket.

Meeting Alan again was a surprise for her too, she
thought, but tricky when she had so many things to
conceal.

'Sorry.' Her smile was swift and genuinely apolo-
getic. 'I have to be somewhere in about five minutes.

'At your husband's beck and call, no doubt.'

She hesitated. 'Actually, Renzo's—away at the moment.'

'Leaving you alone so soon?'

Marisa shrugged. 'Well, we're hardly joined at the hip.' She tried to sound jokey.

'No,' he said. 'I can imagine.' He paused. 'So, what do grass widows do? Count the hours until the errant husband returns?'

'Far from it,' she said crisply. 'They get on with their own lives. Go places and see people.'

'If that's true,' he said slowly, 'maybe you'd consider seeing me one more time.' His voice deepened urgently. 'Marisa—if lunch is impossible meet me for dinner instead—will you? Eight o'clock at Chez Dominique? For old times' sake?'

She wanted to tell him that the old times were over. That they'd died the day he had allowed himself to be shunted out of her life and off to Hong Kong, because he hadn't been prepared to fight for her against a man who was powerful enough to kill his career with a word.

Not that she could altogether blame him, she reminded herself. Their romance had been at far too early a stage to command the kind of loyalty and commitment that she'd needed. It had only amounted to a few kisses, for heaven's sake. And it was one of those kisses that had brought their relationship to a premature end—when Alan had been caught saying goodnight to her by Cousin Julia.

That tense, shocking night when she'd finally discovered what the future really had in store for her.

If Alan had really been my lover, she thought, *I wouldn't have been a virgin bride, and therefore there'd have been no marriage to Renzo. But I—I didn't realise that until it was too late. Alan had already left, and, anyway, did I ever truly care enough for him to give myself in that way?*

She concealed a shiver as unwanted memories stirred. Lingered disturbingly. 'Alan—about tonight—I don't know… And I really must go now.'

'I'll book the table,' he said. 'And wait. Everything else is up to you.'

She gave him an uncertain smile. 'Well, whatever happens, it's been good to see you again.' And hurried away.

She was back at the gallery right on time, but Corin was hovering anxiously nevertheless, the coming session with his lawyers clearly at the forefront of his mind.

'He's going through a difficult divorce,' Dinah had warned her. 'The major problem being that he's still in love with his wife, whereas her only interest is establishing how many of his assets she can take into her new relationship. So he occasionally needs a shoulder to cry on.' She'd paused delicately. 'Think you can manage that?'

'Of course,' Marisa had returned robustly. She might even be able to pick up a few pointers for her own divorce when it became legally viable, she'd thought wryly. Except she wanted nothing from her brief, ill-starred marriage except her freedom. A view that she hoped Lorenzo Santangeli would share.

'I'd better be off,' Corin said, then paused at the doorway. 'If Mrs Brooke rings about that water-colour…'

'The price remains exactly the same.' Marisa smiled at him. 'Don't worry—I won't let her argue me down. Now go, or you'll be late.'

'Yes,' he said, and sighed heavily. 'I suppose so.'

She watched him standing on the kerb, raking a worried hand through his hair as he hailed a cab. And he had every reason to appear harassed, she mused. The former Mrs Langford had not only demanded the marital home, but was also claiming a major share in the gallery too, on the grounds that her father had con-tributed much of the initial financial backing.

'My father and hers were friends,' Dinah had confided. 'And Dad says he'd be spinning in his grave if he knew what Janine was up to. If she gets her hands on the Estrello it will be closed, and Corin will be out by the end of the year.'

'But it's very successful,' Marisa pointed out, startled. 'He's a terrific businessman, and his clients obviously trust him.'

Dinah snorted. 'You think she cares about that? No way. All she can see is a valuable piece of real estate. As soon as her father died she was badgering Corin to sell, and when he wouldn't she decided to end the marriage—as soon as she found someone to take his place.' She added, 'He doesn't deserve it, of course. But—as the saying goes—nice guys finish last.'

Yes, Marisa had thought bitterly, and bastards like Lorenzo Santangeli spend their lives in pole position. There's no justice.

Feeling suddenly restive, she walked over to her desk and sat down, reaching determinedly for the small pile of paperwork that Corin had left for her. It might not be much, she thought wryly, but at least it would stop her mind straying down forbidden pathways.

The afternoon wasn't particularly busy, but it was profitable, as people came in to buy rather than simply browse. A young couple seeking a wedding present for friends bought a pair of modern miniatures, Mrs Brooke reluctantly agreed to buy the watercolour at full price, and an elderly man eventually decided to acquire a Lake District landscape for his wife's birthday.

'We went there on our honeymoon,' he confided to Marisa as she dealt with his credit card payment. 'However, I admit I was torn between that and the wonderful view of the Italian coastline by the same artist.' He sighed reminiscently. 'We've spent several holidays around Amalfi, and it would have brought back a lot of happy memories.' He paused. 'Do you know the area at all?'

For a moment Marisa's fingers froze, and she nearly bodged the transaction. But she forced herself to concentrate, smiling stiltedly as she handed him his card and receipt. 'I have been there, yes. Just once. It—it's incredibly beautiful.'

And I wish you had bought that painting instead, because then I would never—ever—have to look at it again.

She arranged a date and time for delivery of his purchase, and saw him to the door.

Back at her desk, entering the final details of the deal into the computer, she found herself stealing covert looks over her shoulder to the place on the wall where the Amalfi scene was still hanging.

It was as if, she thought, the artist had also visited the Casa Adriana and sat in its lush, overgrown garden on the stone bench in the shade of the lemon tree. As if he too had looked over the crumbling wall to where the rugged cliff tumbled headlong down to the exquisite azure ripple of the Gulf of Salerno far below.

From the moment she'd seen the painting she'd felt the breath catch painfully in her throat. Because it was altogether too potent a reminder of her hiding place—her sanctuary—during those seemingly endless, agonising weeks that had been her honeymoon. The place that, once found, she'd retreated to each morning, knowing that no one would be looking for her, or indeed would find her, and where she'd discovered that solitude did not have to mean loneliness as she shakily counted down the days that would decide her immediate fate.

The place that she'd left each evening as sunset approached, forcing her to return once more to the cold, taut silence of the Villa Santa Caterina and the reluctant company of the man she'd married, to dine with him in the warm darkness at a candlelit table on a flower-hung terrace, where every waft of scented air had seemed, in unconscious irony, to breathe a soft but powerful sexuality.

And where, when the meal had finally ended, she would wish him a quiet goodnight, formally returned, and go off to lie alone in the wide bed with its snowy sheets, praying that her bedroom door would not open because, in spite of everything, boredom or impatience might drive him to seek her out again.

But thankfully it had never happened, and now they were apart without even the most fleeting of contact between them any longer. Presumably, she thought, biting her lip, Renzo had taken the hint, and all that remained now was for him to take the necessary steps to bring their so-called marriage to an end.

I should never have agreed to it in the first place, she told herself bitterly. *I must have been mad. But whatever I thought of Cousin Julia I couldn't deliberately see her made homeless, especially with a sick husband on her hands.*

She'd been embarrassed when Julia had walked into the drawing room that night and found her in Alan's arms, but embarrassment had soon turned to outrage when her cousin, with a smile as bleak as

Antarctica, had insisted that he leave and, in spite of her protests, ushered Alan out of the drawing room and to the front door.

'How dared you do that?' Marisa had challenged, her voice shaking when Julia returned alone. 'I'm not a child any more, and I'm entitled to see anyone I wish.'

Julia had shaken her head. 'I'm afraid not, my dear—precisely because you're not a child any more.' She'd paused, her lips stretching into a thin smile. 'You see, your future husband doesn't want any other man poaching on his preserves—something that was made more than clear when I originally agreed to be your guardian. So we'll pretend this evening never happened—shall we? I promise you it will be much the best thing for both of us.'

There had been, Marisa remembered painfully, a long silence. Then her own voice saying, 'The best thing? What on earth are you talking about? I—I don't have any future husband. It's nonsense.'

'Oh, don't be naive,' her cousin tossed back at her contemptuously. 'You know as well as I do that you're expected to marry Lorenzo Santangeli. It was all arranged years ago.'

Marisa felt suddenly numb. 'Marry—Renzo? But that was never serious,' she managed through dry lips. 'It—it was just one of those silly things that people say.'

'On the contrary, my dear, it's about as serious as it can get.' Julia sat down. 'The glamorous Signor

Santangeli has merely been waiting for you to reach an appropriate age before making you his bride.'

Marisa's throat tightened. She said curtly, 'Now, that I don't believe.'

'It is probably an exaggeration,' Julia agreed. 'I doubt if he's given you a thought from one year's end to another. But he's remembered you now, or had his memory jogged for him, so he's paying us a visit in a week or two in order to stake his claim.' She gave a mocking whistle. 'Rich, good-looking, and a tiger in the sack, by all accounts. Congratulations, my pet. You've won the jackpot.'

'I've won nothing.' Marisa's heart was hammering painfully. 'Because it's not going to happen. My God, I don't even *like* him.'

'Well, he's hardly cherishing a hidden passion for you either,' Julia Gratton said crushingly. 'It's an arranged marriage, you silly little bitch, not a love match. The Santangeli family need a young, healthy girl to provide them with the next generation, and you're their choice.'

'Then they'll have to look elsewhere.' Marisa's voice trembled. 'Because I'm not for sale.'

'My dear child,' Julia drawled. 'You were bought and paid for years ago.' She gestured around her. 'How do you imagine we can afford to live in this house, rather than the one-bedroom nightmare Harry and I were renting when your parents died? Where did your school fees come from? And who's been keeping the roof over our heads and feeding us all, as well as providing the money for your clothes, holidays and various amusements?'

'I thought—you…'

'Don't be a fool. Harry edits academic books. He's hardly coining it in. And now that he has multiple sclerosis he won't be able to work at all for much longer.'

Marisa flung back her head. She said hoarsely, 'I'll get a job. Pay them back every penny.'

'Doing what?' Julia demanded derisively. 'Apart from this part-time course in fine arts you're following at the moment, you're trained for nothing except the career that's already mapped out for you—as the wife of a multimillionaire and the mother of his children. It's payback time, and you're the only currency they'll accept.'

'I don't believe it. I won't.' Marisa's voice was urgent. 'Renzo can't have agreed to this. He—he doesn't want me either. I—I know that.'

Julia's laugh was cynical. 'He's a man, my dear, and you're an attractive, nubile girl. He won't find his role as bridegroom too arduous, believe me. He'll fulfil his obligations to his family, and enjoy them too.'

Marisa said slowly, 'That's—obscene.'

'It's the way of the world, my child.' Julia shrugged. 'And life with the future Marchese Santangeli will have other compensations, you know. Once you've given Lorenzo his heir and a spare, I don't imagine you'll see too much of him. He'll continue to amuse himself as he does now, but with rather more discretion, and you'll be left to your own devices.'

Marisa stared at her. She said huskily, 'You mean he's involved with someone? He—has a girlfriend?'

'Oh, she's rather more than that,' Julia said negligently. 'A beautiful Venetian, I understand, called Lucia Gallo, who works in television. They've been quite inseparable for several months.'

'I see.' Instinct told Marisa that her cousin was enjoying this, so she did her best to sound casual. 'Well, if that's the case, why doesn't he marry her instead?'

'Because she's a divorcee, and unsuitable in all kinds of ways.' She paused. 'I thought I'd already indicated that Santangeli brides are expected to come to their marriages as virgins.'

Marisa said coolly, 'But presumably the same rule doesn't apply to the men?'

Julia laughed. 'Hardly. And you'll be glad of that when the time comes, believe me.' Her tone changed, becoming a touch more conciliatory. 'Think about it, Marisa. This marriage won't be all bad news. You've always said you wanted to travel. Well, you'll be able to—and first-class all the way. Or, with Florence on your doorstep, you could always plunge back into the art world. Create your own life.'

'And *that* is supposed to make it all worthwhile?' Marisa queried incredulously. 'I allow myself to be—used—in return for a couple of visits to the Accademia? I won't do it.'

'I think you will,' her cousin said with grim emphasis. 'We're Santangeli pensioners, my pet, all of us. Yourself included. We owe our lifestyle to their goodwill. And once you're married to Lorenzo, that happy state of affairs will continue for Harry and myself. Because they've agreed that we can move out of London to a bungalow, specially adapted for a wheelchair, and employ full-time care when the need arises.' For a moment her voice wavered. 'Something we could never afford to do under normal circumstances.'

She rallied, her tone harsh again. 'But if you try and back out now, the whole thing will crash and burn. We'll lose this house—everything. And I won't see Harry's precarious future in jeopardy because a spoiled little brat who's spent the past few years grabbing everything going with both hands, has suddenly decided the price is too high for her delicate sensibilities. Well, there's no such thing as a free lunch, sweetie, so make the best of it.

'And remember, a lot of girls would kill to be in your shoes. So, if nothing else, learn to be civil to him in the daytime, co-operate at night, and don't ask awkward questions when he's away. Even you should be able to manage that.'

Except I didn't, Marisa thought wearily, shivering as she remembered the note of pure vitriol in her cousin's voice. I failed on every single count.

She sighed. She'd fought—of course she had— using every conceivable argument against the unwanted marriage. She'd also spent the next few days trying to contact Alan, who had been strangely unavailable.

And when at last she had managed to speak to him on the phone, over a week later, she'd learned that he'd been offered a transfer, with promotion, to Hong Kong, and would be leaving almost at once.

'It's a great opportunity,' he told her, his voice uncomfortable. 'And totally unexpected. I could have waited years for something like this.'

'I see.' Her mind was whirling, but she kept her tone light. 'I suppose you wouldn't consider taking me with you?'

There was a silence, then he said jerkily, 'Marisa— you know that isn't going to happen. Neither of us are free agents in this. I know that strings were pulled to get me this job because you're soon moving to a different league.' He paused. 'I don't think I'm really meant to be talking to you now.'

'No,' she said, past the shocked tightness in her throat. 'Probably not. And I—I quite understand. Well—good luck.'

After that it had been difficult to go on fighting, once her stunned mind had registered that she had no one to turn to, nowhere to go, and, as Julia had reminded her, barely enough academic qualifications to earn her a living wage.

But in the end she'd wearily capitulated because of Harry, the quiet, kind man who'd made Julia's reluctant guardianship of her so much more bearable, and who was going to need the Santangeli generosity so badly, and so soon.

But if Renzo Santangeli believed she was going to fall gratefully at his feet, he could think again, she had told herself with icy bitterness.

It was a stance she'd maintained throughout what she supposed had passed for his courtship of her. Admittedly, with the result a foregone conclusion, he hadn't had to try too hard, and she'd been glad of it, reflecting defiantly that the less she saw of him the better. But the fact remained that her avowed resolve had not actually been tested.

The only time she'd really been alone with him before the wedding, she thought, staring at the screensaver on her computer, was when he'd made that strange, almost diffident proposal of marriage, explaining that he wanted to make their difficult situation as easy as possible for her, and that he would force no physical intimacies on her until she'd become accustomed to her new circumstances and was ready to be his wife in every sense of the word.

And as far as their engagement went, he'd kept his word. She hadn't been subjected to any unwelcome advances from him.

No doubt he'd secretly believed he wouldn't have to wait too long, she decided, her mouth tightening.

He'd been sure curiosity alone would undermine her determination to keep him at arm's length, or further.

Well, he'd learned better during the misery of their honeymoon, and their parting at the end of it had come as a relief to them both. And, although he'd made various dutiful attempts to maintain minimal contact with her once she'd moved back to London, he clearly hadn't seen any necessity to try and heal the rift between them in person. Not that she'd have allowed that, anyway, she assured herself hastily.

So, now he seemed to have tacitly accepted that, apart from the inevitable legal formalities, their brief, ill-starred marriage was permanently over. Soon he'd be free to seek a more willing lady to share the marital bed with him when he felt inclined—probably some doe-eyed Italian beauty with a talent for maternity.

Which would certainly please his old witch of a grandmother, who'd made no secret of her disapproval of his chosen match from the moment Marisa had arrived back in Italy under Julia's eagle-eyed escort. Harry had not accompanied them, having opted to spend the time quietly at his sister's home in Kent, but he'd announced his determination to fly out for the wedding in order to give the bride away.

But Renzo's next wooing would almost certainly be conducted in a very different manner.

She'd wondered sometimes if it had been obvious to everyone that he'd rarely touched her, apart from taking her hand when making introductions. And that he'd never kissed her in any way.

Except once…

It had been during the dinner his father had given at the house in Tuscany for her nineteenth birthday, with a large ebullient crowd of family and friends gathered round the long table in the sumptuous frescoed dining room. She'd been seated next to him in her pale cream dress, with its long sleeves and discreetly square neckline, the epitome of the demure *fidanzata*, with the lustrous pearls that had been his birthday gift to her clasped round her throat for everyone to see and admire.

'Pearls for purity,' had been Julia's acid comment when she saw them. 'And costing a fortune too. Clearly he'll be expecting his money's worth on his wedding night.'

Was that the message he was intending to convey to the world at large? Marisa had wondered, wincing. She'd been sorely tempted to put the gleaming string back in its velvet box, but eventually she'd steeled herself to wear it, along with the ring he'd given her to mark their engagement—a large and exquisite ruby surrounded by diamonds.

She could not, she'd thought, fault his generosity in material matters. In fact she'd been astonished when she'd discovered the allowance he proposed to make her when they were married, and could not imagine how she'd spend even a quarter of it.

But then, as she had reminded herself, he was buying her goodwill and, as Julia had so crudely indicated, her body.

It was a thought that had still had the ability to dry her mouth in panic, especially with the wedding drawing closer each day.

Because, in spite of his promised forbearance, there would come a night when she would have to undergo the ordeal of submission to him. 'Payback time', as Julia had called it, and it scared her.

He scared her...

She had turned her head, studying him covertly from under her lashes. He'd been talking to the people across the table, his hands moving incisively to under-line a point, his dark face vivid with laughter, and it had occurred to her, as swiftly and shockingly as a thunderbolt crashing through the ceiling, that if she'd met him that night for the first time she might well have found him deeply and disturbingly attractive.

His lean good looks had been emphasised by the severe formality of dinner jacket and black tie. But then, she'd been forced to admit, he always dressed well, and his clothes were beautiful.

But fast on the heels of that reluctant admission had come another thought that she'd found even more unwelcome.

That, only too soon, she would know what Renzo looked like without any clothes at all.

The breath had caught in her throat, and she'd felt

an odd wave of heat sweep up over her body and turn her face to flame.

And as if he'd picked up her sudden confusion on some secret male radar, Renzo had turned and looked at her, his brows lifting in enquiry as he observed her hectically flushed cheeks and startled eyes.

And for one brief moment they had seemed caught together within a cone of silence, totally cut off from the chatter and laughter around them, his gaze meshing with hers, only to sharpen into surprise and—oh, God—amused awareness.

Making her realise with utter mortification that he'd read her thoughts as easily as if she'd had *I wonder what he looks like naked?* tattooed across her forehead.

He had inclined his head slightly in acknowledgement, the golden eyes dancing, his mouth twisting in mocking appreciation, and reached for the hand that wore his ring, raising her fingers for the brush of his lips, then turning them so he could plant a more deliberate kiss in the softness of her palm.

Her colour had deepened helplessly as she'd heard the ripple of delighted approbation from round the table, and she had known his gesture had been noted.

And she had no one to blame for that but herself, she'd thought, her heart hammering within the prim confines of the cream bodice as she had removed her hand from his clasp with whatever dignity she could salvage. She had known, as she did so, that the guests would be approving of that too, respecting what they saw as her modesty and shyness, when in reality she wanted to grab the nearest wine bottle and break it over his head.

When the dinner had finally ended, an eternity later, she'd been thankful that courtesy kept Renzo with the departing guests, enabling her to escape upstairs without speaking to him.

Julia, however, had not been so easily evaded.

'So,' she said, following Marisa into her bedroom and draping herself over the arm of the little brocaded sofa by the window. 'You seem to be warming at last to your future husband.'

Marisa put the pearls carefully in their case. 'Appearances can be deceptive.'

'Then you're a fool,' her cousin said bluntly. 'He may be charming, but underneath there's one tough individual, and you can't afford to play games with him—blushing and sighing one minute, and becoming an ice maiden the next.'

'Thank you,' Marisa returned politely. 'I'll bear that in mind.'

She'd momentarily lost ground tonight, and she knew it, but it was only a temporary aberration. She'd find a way to make up for it—somehow.

And so I did, she thought now, *only to find myself reaping a bitter harvest as a consequence.*

Her reverie was interrupted by the return of Corin, looking woebegone.

'She wants her half-share in the gallery,' he announced without preamble. 'She says that I'm far too conventional, and she's planning to take an active part in the place—imposing some ideas of her own to widen the customer base. Which means she'll be working next to me every day as if nothing's happened. Well, it's impossible. I couldn't bear it.'

He sat down heavily at his desk. 'Besides, I know her ideas of old, and they just wouldn't work—not somewhere like this. But I can't afford to buy her out,' he added, sighing, 'so I'll just have to sell up and start again—perhaps in some country area where property isn't so expensive.'

Marisa brought him some strong black coffee. She said, 'Couldn't you find a white knight— someone who'd invest in the Estrello so you could pay your wife off?'

He pulled a face. 'If only. But times are bad, and getting harder, and luxury items like these are usually the first to be sacrificed, so I could struggle to find someone willing to take the risk. Anyway, investors generally want more of an instant return than I can offer.'

He savoured a mouthful of his coffee. 'I may close up early tonight,' he went on, giving her a hopeful look. 'Maybe we could have dinner together?'

I'm sorry, Corin, she thought. *But I'm not in the mood to provide a shoulder for you to cry on this evening—or whatever else you might have in mind.*

You're a nice guy, but it stops at lunch. And it stops now. Because I have issues of my own that I should deal with.

Aloud, she said gently, 'I'm sorry, but I already have a date.'

She hadn't intended to meet Alan either, of course, but it had suddenly come to seem a better idea than sitting alone in her flat, brooding about the past.

That's a loser's game, she told herself with determination, *and I need to look to the future—and freedom.*

CHAPTER THREE

EVEN as she was getting dressed for her dinner date with Alan, Marisa was still unsure if she was doing the right thing.

It occurred to her, wryly, that even though it was barely a year since she'd actually contemplated running away with him her heart was not exactly beating faster as she contemplated the evening ahead.

And she hadn't promised to meet him, so ducking out would be an easy option.

On the other hand, going out to a restaurant appeared marginally more tempting than spending another solitary night in front of the television.

Yet solitary, she thought with a faint sigh, *is what I seem to do best.*

Up to now, having her own place for the first time in her life had felt a complete bonus. Admittedly, with only one bedroom, it wasn't the biggest flat in the world—in fact, it could have been slipped inside the Santangeli house in Tuscany and lost—but it was light, bright, well furnished, with a well-fitted kitchen and shower room, and was sited in a smart, modern block of similar apartments in an upmarket area of London.

Best of all, living there, as she often reminded herself, she answered to no one.

There was, naturally, a downside. She had to accept that her independence had its limits, because she didn't actually pay the rent. That was taken care of by a firm of lawyers, acting as agents for her husband.

After the divorce was finalised, she realised, she would no longer be able to afford anything like it.

Her life would also be subject to all kinds of other changes, not many of them negative. In spite of Julia's dismissive words, her academic results had been perfectly respectable, and she hadn't understood at the time why she'd received no encouragement to seek qualifications in some form of higher education, like her classmates.

How naive was it possible to get? she wondered, shaking her head in self-derision.

However, there was nothing to prevent her doing so in the future, with the help of a student loan. She could even look on the time she'd spent as Renzo's wife as a kind of 'gap year', she told herself, her mouth twisting.

And now she had the immediate future to deal with, in the shape of this evening, which might also have its tricky moments unless she was vigilant. After all, the last thing she wanted was for Alan to think she was a lonely wife in need of consolation.

Because nothing could be further from the truth.

She picked out her clothes with care—a pale blue denim wrap-around skirt topped by a white silk shirt—hoping her choice wouldn't look as if she was trying too hard. Then, proceeding along the same lines, she applied a simple dusting of powder to her face, and the lightest touch of colour on her mouth.

Lastly, and with reluctance, she retrieved her wedding ring from the box hidden in her dressing table and slid it on to her finger. She hadn't planned to wear it again, but its presence on her hand would be a tacit reminder to her companion that the evening was a one-off and she was certainly not available— by any stretch of the imagination.

Two hours later, she was ruefully aware that Alan's thinking had not grown any more elastic during his absence, and that, in spite of the romantic ambience that Chez Dominique had always cultivated, she was having a pretty dull evening.

A faintly baffling one, too, because he seemed to be in a nostalgic mood, talking about their past relationship as if it had been altogether deeper and more meaningful than she remembered.

Get a grip, she thought, irritated. *You may have been a few years older than I was, but we were still hardly more than boy and girl. I was certainly a virgin, and I suspect you probably were too, although that's almost certainly no longer true for either of us.*

He had far more confidence these days, smartly

dressed in a light suit, with a blue shirt that matched his eyes. And he seemed to have had his slightly crooked front teeth fixed too.

All in all, she decided, he was a nice guy. But that was definitely as far as it went.

However, the food at Chez Dominique was still excellent, and when she managed to steer him away from personal issues and on to his life in Hong Kong she became rather more interested in what he had to say, and was able to feel glad that he was doing well.

But even so, the fact that he had not gone there through choice clearly still rankled with him, and although he'd probably bypassed a rung or two on the corporate ladder as a result of his transfer, she detected that there was a note of resentment never far from the surface.

As the waiter brought his cheese and her *crème brûlée*, Alan said, 'Are you staying with your cousin while you're in London?'

'Oh, no,' Marisa returned, without thinking. 'Julia lives near Tonbridge Wells these days.'

'You mean you've actually been allowed off the leash without a minder?' His tone was barbed. 'Amazing.'

'Not particularly.' She ate some of her dessert. 'Perhaps—Lorenzo—' she stumbled slightly over the name '—trusts me.' *Or he simply doesn't care what I do...*

'So I suppose you must have a suite at the Ritz, or some other five-star palace?' He gave a small bitter laugh. 'How the other half live.'

'Nothing of the sort,' Marisa said tersely. 'I'm actually using someone's flat.' Which was, she thought, an approximation of the truth, and also a reminder of how very much she wanted to get back there and avoid answering any more of the questions that he was obviously formulating over his Port Salut.

She glanced at her watch and gave a controlled start. 'Heavens, is that really the time? I should be going.'

'Expecting a phone call from the absent husband?' There was a faintly petulant note in his voice.

'No,' she said. 'I have an early appointment tomorrow.' *At my desk in the Estrello, at nine o'clock sharp.*

At the same time she was aware that his remark had made her freeze inwardly. Because there'd been a time, she thought, when Renzo had called her nearly every day, coming up each time against the deliberate barrier of her answering machine, and leaving increasingly brief and stilted messages, which she had deleted as quickly as she'd torn up his unread letters.

Until the night when he'd said abruptly, an odd almost raw note in his voice, 'Tomorrow, Marisa, when I call you, please pick up the phone. There are things that need to be said.' He'd paused, then added, 'I beg you to do this.'

And when the phone had rung the following night she'd been shocked to find that she'd almost had to sit on her hands to prevent herself from lifting the receiver. That she'd had to repeat silently to herself over and over again, *There is nothing he can say that I could possibly want to hear.*

Then, in the silence of all the evenings that followed, she had come to realise that he was not going to call again, and that her intransigence had finally achieved the victory she wanted. And she had found she was wondering why her triumph suddenly seemed so sterile.

Something, she thought, she had still not managed to work out to her own satisfaction.

She had a polite tussle with Alan over her share of the bill, which he won, and walked out into the street with a feeling of release. She turned to say goodnight and found him at the kerb, hailing a taxi, which was thoughtful.

But she hadn't bargained for him clambering in after her.

She said coolly, 'Oh—may I drop you somewhere?'

He smiled at her. 'I was hoping you might offer me some coffee—or a nightcap.'

Her heart sank like a stone. 'It is getting late...'

'Not too late, surely—for old times' sake?'

He was over-fond of that phrase, Marisa decided irritably. And his 'old times' agenda clearly differed substantially from hers.

She said, not bothering to hide her reluctance, 'Well—a quick coffee, perhaps, and then you must go,' and watched with foreboding as his smile deepened into satisfaction.

She didn't doubt her ability to keep him at bay. She had, after all, done it before, with someone else, even though it had rebounded on her later in a way that still had the power to turn her cold all over at the memory.

But she told herself grimly, Alan was a totally different proposition. She'd make sure that when he'd drunk his coffee he would go away and stay away. There'd be no more meetings during this leave or any other.

As they went up in the lift to the second floor of the apartment block she was aware he'd moved marginally closer. She stepped back, deliberately distancing herself and hoping he'd take the hint.

But as she turned the key in the lock he was standing so close behind her that his breath was stirring her hair, and she flung the door open, almost jumping across the narrow hallway into the living room.

Where, she realised with shock, the light was on.

Also—the room was occupied.

She stopped so abruptly that Alan nearly cannoned into her as she saw with horror exactly who was waiting for her.

Lorenzo Santangeli was lounging full-length on the sofa, totally at ease, jacket and tie removed, with his white shirt unbuttoned almost to the waist, its sleeves turned back over his bronze forearms.

An opened bottle of red wine and two glasses, one half-filled, stood on the low table in front of the sofa.

As she stood, gaping at him, he smiled at her,

tossed aside the book he was reading and swung his legs to the floor.

'Maria Lisa,' he said softly. *'Carissima.* You have returned at last. I was becoming worried about you.'

Throat dry with disbelief, she found a voice from somewhere. 'Renzo—I—I…' She gulped a breath, and formed words that made sense. 'What are you doing here?'

'I wished to surprise you, my sweet.' His voice was silky. 'And I see that I have done so.' He walked to her on bare feet, took her nerveless hand, and raised it briefly and formally to his lips before looking past her. With a feeling of total unreality she saw that he needed a shave.

He went on, 'Will you not introduce me to your escort, and allow me to thank him for bringing you safely to your door?'

In the ensuing silence she heard Alan swallow— deafeningly. Got herself somehow under control.

She said quietly, 'Of course. This is Alan Denison, an old friend, home on leave from Hong Kong.' *And he seems to have turned the most odd shade of green. I didn't know people really did that.*

For a moment she thought she saw a swift flicker of surprise in Renzo's astonishing golden eyes. Then he said smoothly, 'Ah, yes—I recall.'

'We just—happened to run into each other.' Alan spoke hoarsely. 'In the street. This morning. And I asked your—Signora Santangeli—to have dinner with me.'

'A kind thought,' Renzo returned. He was still, Marisa realised, holding her hand. And instinct warned her not to pull away. Not this time.

All the same, he was far too close for comfort. She was even aware of the faint, beguiling scent of the cologne he used, and her throat tightened at the unwanted memories it evoked.

Alan began to back towards the door. If she hadn't been in such turmoil, Marisa could almost have found it funny. As it was, she wanted to scream, *Don't go.*

He babbled on, 'But now I can safely leave her in your...' He paused.

Oh, God, Marisa thought hysterically, please don't say *capable hands*.

But to her relief, Alan only added lamely, 'In your care.'

Which was quite bad enough, given the circumstances.

'You are all consideration, *signore*. Permit me to wish you goodnight—on my wife's behalf as well as my own.' Keeping Marisa firmly at his side, Renzo watched expressionlessly as the younger man muttered something incomprehensible in reply, then fumbled his way out of the flat, closing the door behind him.

Once they were alone, she wrenched herself free and stepped back, distancing herself deliberately, her heart hammering against her ribcage.

As she made herself meet Renzo's enigmatic gaze, she said defensively, 'It's not what you think.'

The dark brows lifted. 'You have become a mind-reader during our separation, *mia cara*?'

'No.' It was her turn to swallow. 'But—but I know how it must look.'

'I know that he looked disappointed,' Renzo returned pleasantly. 'That told me all that was necessary. And you are far too young to claim a man as an old friend,' he added, clicking his tongue reprovingly. 'It lacks—credibility.'

She drew a deep breath. 'When I want your advice I'll ask for it. And Alan and I *were* friends—until you stepped in. Also,' she went on, defiantly bending the truth, 'he came back here this evening at my invitation—for coffee. That's all. So please don't judge other people by your own dubious standards.'

He looked at her with amusement. 'I see that absence has not sweetened your tongue, *mia bella*.'

'Well, you're not obliged to listen to it,' she said raggedly. 'And what the hell are you doing here, anyway? How dare you walk in and—make yourself at home like this?'

Renzo casually resumed his seat on the sofa, leaning back against its cushions as if he belonged there. He said gently, 'Not the warmest of welcomes, *mia cara*. And we are husband and wife, so your home is also mine. Where else should I be?'

Marisa lifted her chin. 'I'd say that was an open question.' A thought occurred to her. 'And how did you get in, may I ask?'

Renzo shrugged. 'The apartment is leased in my name, so naturally I have a key.'

There was a silence, then she said jerkily, 'I—I see. I suppose I should have realised that.'

He watched her, standing near the door, her white cotton jacket still draped across her shoulders. His mouth twisted. 'You look poised for flight, Maria Lisa,' he commented. 'Where are you planning to go?'

Her glance was mutinous. 'Somewhere that you won't find me.'

'You think there is such a place?' He shook his head slowly. 'I, on the other hand, think it is time for us to sit down and talk together like civilised people.'

'Hardly an accurate description of our relationship to date,' she said. 'And I'd actually prefer you to be the one to leave.' She marched to the door and flung it wide. 'You got rid of Alan, *signore*. I suggest you follow him.'

'A telling gesture,' he murmured. 'But sadly wasted. Because I am going nowhere. I came here because there are things to be said. So why don't you sit down and drink some wine with me?'

'Because I don't want any wine,' she said mutinously. 'And if there's any talking to be done it should be through lawyers. They can make all the necessary arrangements.'

He stretched indolently, making her tinglingly and indignantly aware of every lean inch of him. 'What arrangements are those?'

'Please don't play games,' she said shortly. 'Our divorce, naturally.'

'There has never been a divorce in the Santangeli family,' Renzo said quietly. 'And mine will not be the first. We are married, Maria Lisa, and that is how I intend us to remain.'

He paused, observing the angry colour draining from her face, then added, 'You surely cannot have believed that I intended this period of separation to be permanent?'

She looked at him defiantly. 'I certainly hoped so.'

'Then you will have to preserve your optimism until death parts us, *carissima*.' His tone held finality. 'This was a breathing space, no more than that.' He paused. 'As I made clear, though you may have chosen to think otherwise. But it makes no difference. You are still my wife, and you always will be.'

Her hands were clenched at her sides, the folds of her skirt concealing the fact that they were trembling.

'Is that what you've come here to tell me—that I can never be free of you, *signore*? But that's ridiculous. We can't go on living like this. You can't possibly want that any more than I do.'

'For once we are in agreement,' he said softly. 'Perhaps it is a good omen.'

'Don't count on it.'

His mouth twisted. 'With you, Maria Lisa, I count on nothing, believe me. *Tuttavia*, I am here to invite you to return to Italy and take your place beside me.'

For a moment she stared at him, appalled, and then she said, 'No! You can't. I—I won't.'

He poured more wine into his glass and drank. 'May I ask why not?'

She stared down at the carpet. She said huskily, 'I think you know the answer to that already.'

'Ah,' he said. 'You mean you are still not prepared to forgive me for the mistakes of our honeymoon. Yet even you must admit they were not completely one-sided, *mia cara*.'

'You can hardly blame me,' she flashed. 'After all, I promised you nothing.'

'Then you were entirely true to yourself, *mia bella*, because you gave nothing,' Renzo bit back at her. 'And you cannot pretend you did not know the terms of our marriage.'

'No, but I didn't expect they'd be exacted in that particular way.'

'And I did not expect my patience to be tried so sorely, or so soon.' His golden gaze met hers in open challenge. 'Maybe we have both learned something from that unhappy time.'

'Yes,' Marisa's voice was stony. 'I have discovered you can't be trusted, and that's why I won't be going with you to Italy, or anywhere else. I want out of this so-called marriage, *signore*, and nothing you can say or do will change my mind.'

'Not even,' he said slowly, 'when I tell you my father is sick and has been asking for you?'

She came forward slowly and sat down on the edge of the chair opposite, staring at him. She said shakily, 'Zio Guillermo—sick?' She shook her head. 'I don't believe you. He's never had a day's illness in his life.'

'Nevertheless, he suffered a heart attack two nights ago.' His tone was bleak. 'As you may imagine, it was a shock to both of us. And now to you also, perhaps.'

'Oh, God. Yes, of course. I can see…' Her voice tailed away in distress. She was silent for a moment, then moistened her dry lips with the tip of her tongue. 'Poor Zio Guillermo. Is it—very bad?'

'No,' he said. 'He has been very fortunate—this time. You see that I am being honest with you,' he added, his mouth curling sardonically. 'At the moment his life is not threatened. But he has to rest and avoid stress, which is not easy when our marriage continues to be a cause of such great concern to him.'

She'd been gazing downwards, but at that her head lifted sharply. She said, 'That's—blackmail.'

'If you wish to think so.' Renzo shrugged. 'Unfortunately, it is also the truth. Papa fears he will not live to see his grandchildren.' His eyes met hers. 'He does not deserve such a disappointment, Maria Lisa— from either of us. So I say it is time we fulfilled the terms of our agreement and made him a happy man.'

She stared back at him. She said, in a small, wrenched whisper, 'You mean you're going to—force me to have your child?'

He moved suddenly, restively. 'I shall enforce

nothing.' His tone was harsh. 'I make you that promise. What I am asking is your forgiveness for the past, a chance to make amends to you—and begin our life together again. To see if we can at least become friends in this marriage, if nothing else.'

Marisa sank her teeth into her bottom lip. 'But you'll still want me to do—*that.*'

His mouth hardened. *'That,'* he said, 'is how babies are made.' He paused, then added quietly, 'It is also how love is made.'

'Not a word,' Marisa said, icily, 'that could ever be applied to our situation.'

He shrugged cynically. 'Yet a girl does not have to be in love with a man to enjoy what he does to her in bed. Did your charming cousin not mention that in her pre-marital advice?' He saw the colour mount in her face and nodded. 'I see that she did.'

She said curtly, 'It is not an opinion that I happen to share.'

'And were you hoping for a more romantic en-counter tonight, which I have spoiled by my untimely arrival?' His smile did not reach his eyes. 'My poor Marisa, *ti devo delle scuse.* You have so much to forgive me for.'

Her glance held defiance. 'But not for this evening— which was a—mistake.' *One of so many I've made...*

'Che sollievo,' he said softly. 'I am relieved to hear it. He paused. 'I have reservations on the afternoon flight tomorrow. I hope you can be ready.'

'I haven't yet said I'll go with you!' There was alarm in her voice.

'True,' he agreed. 'But I hope you will give it serious consideration. However poorly you think of me, Maria Lisa, my father deserves your gratitude and your affection. Your return would give him the greatest pleasure. Can you really begrudge him that?'

She hesitated. 'I could come for a visit…'

He shook his head. 'No, *per sempre*. You stay for good.' His mouth twisted. 'You have to learn to be my wife, *mia bella*. To run the household, manage the servants, treat my father at all times with respect, entertain my friends, and appear beside me in public. This will all take time, although by now it should be as natural to you as breathing. I have waited long enough.'

He paused. 'Also, at some mutually convenient time, you will begin to share my bed. *Capisci?*'

She turned away, saying in a suffocated voice, 'Yes, I—I understand.' She took a deep breath. 'But I can't possibly leave tomorrow. You see—I—I have a job, and I need to give proper notice.'

'Your job at the Estrello Gallery is a temporary one,' Renzo said casually. 'And I am sure Signor Langford will make allowances once he understands the position.'

She swung back, staring at him in stunned silence. At last she said unevenly, 'You—already knew? About my work—everything?' Her voice rose. 'Are you telling me you've been having me *watched*?'

'Naturally,' he returned, shrugging. 'You are my wife, Marisa. I had to make sure that you came to no harm while we were apart.'

'By having me—*spied on*?' She took a quick breath. 'My God, that's despicable.'

'A precaution, no more.' He added softly, 'And with your best interests at heart, *mia cara,* whatever you may think. After all, when you would not answer my letters or return my calls I had to maintain some contact with you.'

She pushed her hair back from her face with a shaking hand. 'I only wish I'd thought of setting detectives on *you*. I bet I'd have all the evidence I need to be rid of this marriage by now.'

He said gently, 'Or perhaps you would find that I am not so easily disposed of.' He poured wine into the second glass and rose, bringing it to her. 'Let us drink a toast, *carissima*. To the future.'

'I can't.' Marisa put her hands behind her back defensively. 'Because I won't be a hypocrite. This is the last thing in the world I was expecting. You—must see that, and you have to give me more time—to think…'

'You have had months to think,' Renzo said. 'And to come to terms with the situation.'

'You make it sound so simple,' she said bitterly.

'You are my wife,' he said. 'I wish you to live with me. It is hardly complicated.'

'But there are so many other girls around.' She swallowed. 'If not a divorce, we could have an annulment. We could say that nothing happened—after all, it hardly did—and then you could choose someone you wanted—who'd want you in return.'

'There is no question of that.' His tone was harsh. 'I have come to take you home, Maria Lisa, and, whether it is given willingly or unwillingly, I shall require your agreement at breakfast tomorrow. No other answer will do.'

'Breakfast?' she repeated, at a loss. 'You mean—you wish me to come to your hotel?'

'You will not be put to so much trouble,' he said. 'I am spending the night here.'

'No!' The word burst from her. 'You—you can't. It's quite impossible.' She paused, swallowing. 'Even you must see that the flat's far too small.'

'You mean that there is only one bedroom and one bed?' he queried with faint amusement. 'I had already discovered that for myself. But it need not be an obstacle.'

She wrapped her arms defensively round her body. 'Oh, yes, it is,' she said, her voice shaking. 'Because I—I won't…' She flung her head back. 'Oh, God, I knew I couldn't trust you.'

'*Calmati!*' His voice bit. 'I am under no illusion, *mia bella*, that I am any more welcome in your bed now than I was on our wedding night. And for the time being I accept the situation. So believe that you are quite safe. *Inoltre*, your sofa seems comfortable enough, if you will spare me a pillow and a blanket.'

She stared at him almost blankly. 'You'll—sleep on the sofa?'

'I have just said so.' His brows lifted. 'Is there some law forbidding it?'

'Oh, no,' Marisa denied hastily. She sighed. 'Well, if—if you're determined to stay, I'll—get what you need. And a towel.'

'*Grazie mille*,' he acknowledged sardonically. 'I hope you will not be so grudging with your hospitality when you are called upon to entertain our guests.'

'Guests,' she said grittily, 'are usually invited. Also welcome.'

'And you cannot imagine that a day might come when you would be glad to see me?' he asked, apparently unfazed.

'Frankly, no.'

'Yet I can recall a time when your feelings for me were not quite so hostile.'

Pain twisted inside her as she remembered how hopelessly—helplessly—she'd once adored him, but she kept her voice icily level. 'The foolishness of adolescence, *signore*.' She shrugged. 'Fortunately it didn't last. Not once I realised what you really were.'

He said reflectively, 'Perhaps we should halt there. I think I would prefer not to enquire into the precise nature of your discovery.'

'Scared of the truth?' Marisa lifted her chin in challenge.

'Not at all,' he said. 'When it *is* the truth.' He looked

at her steadily, his mouth hard. 'But I swore to myself on my mother's memory that I would not lose my temper with you again, whatever the provocation.' He paused significantly. 'Yet there are limits to my tolerance, Maria Lisa. I advise you to observe them, and not push me too far.'

'Why?' She looked down at the floor, aware of a sudden constriction in her breathing. 'What more can you possibly do to me?'

He said quietly, 'I suggest you do not find out,' and there was a note in his voice that sent a shiver the length of her spine. 'Now, perhaps you will fetch me that blanket—*per favore*.'

She was halfway to her room when she realised he was right behind her.

She said, 'You don't have to follow me. I can manage.'

'My travel bag is on your floor,' he said tersely. 'Also I wish to use the shower.'

'You have an answer to everything, don't you?'

He gave her an enigmatic glance. 'Not to you, *mia bella*. That is one of the few certainties in our situation,' he added, bending to retrieve the elegant black leather holdall standing just inside her bedroom door.

And he walked away before she could commit the fatal error of asking what the others might be.

Not that she would have done, of course, Marisa told herself as she extracted a dark red woollen blanket and a towel from the storage drawers under her bed, and took a pillow from a shelf in the fitted wardrobes. She would not give him the satisfaction, she thought, angry to discover that she was trembling inside, and still breathless from their encounter.

But then she was still suffering from shock at having come back and found him there, waiting for her. Waiting, moreover, to stake a claim that she had thought—hoped—had been tacitly forgotten.

She'd actually allowed herself to believe that she was free. To imagine that the respite she'd been offered had become a permanent separation and that, apart from a few legal formalities, their so-called marriage was over.

But she'd just been fooling herself, she thought wretchedly. It was never going to be that easy.

Because as she now realised, too late, they'd never been apart at all in any real sense. Had been, in fact, linked all the time by a kind of invisible rope. And it had only taken one brief, determined tug on Renzo's part to draw her inexorably—inevitably—back to him, to keep the promises she'd made one late August day in a crowded sunlit church.

And of course, to repay some small part of that enormous, suffocating debt to him and his family in the only currency available to her.

She shivered swiftly and uncontrollably.

She could, she supposed, refuse to go back to Italy with him. He was, after all, hardly likely to kidnap her. But even if they remained apart there was no guarantee that the marriage could ever be brought to a legal end. He had made it quite clear that she was his wife, and would continue to be so, and he had the money and the lawyers to enforce his will in this respect, to keep her tied to him with no prospect of release.

The alternative was to take Julia's unsavoury advice. To accede somehow to the resumption of Renzo's physical requirements of her and give him the son he needed. That accomplished, their relationship would presumably exist in name only, and she could then create a whole new life for herself, perhaps. Even find some form of happiness.

She carried the bedding down the hall to the living room, then stopped abruptly on the threshold, her startled gaze absorbing the totally unwelcome sight of Renzo, his shirt discarded, displaying altogether too much bronze skin as he casually unbuckled the belt of his pants.

She said glacially, 'I'd prefer you to change in the bathroom.'

'And I would prefer you to accustom yourself to the reality of having a husband, *mia bella*,' he retorted, with equal coolness. He looked her up and down slowly, his eyes lingering deliberately on the fastening of her skirt. 'Now, if you were to undress in front of me I should have no objection,' he added mockingly.

'Hell,' Marisa said, 'will freeze over first.' She put the armful of bedding down on the carpet and walked away without hurrying.

Yet once in the sanctuary of her bedroom she found

herself leaning back against its panels, gasping for breath as if she'd just run a mile in record time.

Oh, why—*why*—did the lock on this damned door have no key? she wondered wildly. Something that would make her feel safe.

Except that would be a total self-delusion, and she knew it. Because there was no lock, bolt or chain yet invented that would keep Renzo Santangeli at bay if ever he decided that he wanted her.

Instead, she had to face the fact that it was only his indifference that would guarantee her privacy tonight.

A reflection that, to her own bewilderment, gave her no satisfaction at all.

CHAPTER FOUR

THE sofa, Renzo thought bleakly, was not at all as comfortable as he'd claimed.

But even if it had been as soft as a featherbed, and long enough to accommodate his tall frame without difficulty, he would still have found sleep no easier to come by.

Arms folded behind his head, he lay staring up at the faint white sheen of the ceiling, his mind jagged and restless.

He was enough of a realist to have accepted that he wouldn't find a subdued, compliant bride awaiting him in London, but neither had he anticipated quite such a level of intransigence. Had hoped, in fact, that allowing her this time away from him might have brought about a faint softening of her attitude. A basis for negotiation, at least.

But how wrong was it possible to be? he asked himself wryly. It seemed she had no wish either to forgive him—or forget—so any plans he'd been formulating for a fresh start between them were back in the melting pot.

The simplest solution to his problems, of course, would be to settle for the so-called annulment she had offered and walk away. Accept that their marriage had never had a chance of success.

Indeed, the days leading up to the wedding had been almost surreal, with Marisa, like a ghost, disappearing at his approach, and when forced to remain in his presence speaking only when spoken to.

Except once. When for one brief moment at that dinner party he'd discovered her looking at him with a speculation in her eyes there had been no mistaking. And for that moment his heart had lifted in frank jubilation.

He remembered how he hadn't been able to wait for their dinner guests to leave in order to seek her out and invite her to go for a stroll with him in the moonlit privacy of the gardens, telling himself that maybe he was being given a belated opportunity for a little delicate wooing of his reluctant bride, and that, if so, he would take full advantage of it.

But once all the goodnights had been said, and he'd gone to find her, she had retreated to the sanctuary of her room and the chance had gone—especially as he'd had to return to Rome early the following morning.

But he hadn't been able to forget that just for an instant she had lowered her guard. That she had seen him—reacted to him as a man. And that when he'd kissed her hand she'd blushed helplessly.

Which suggested that, if there'd been one chink in her armour, surely he might somehow find another…

So, he was not yet ready to admit defeat, he told himself grimly. He would somehow persuade her to agree to erase the past and accept him as her husband. A resolve that had been hardened by his unwanted interview with his grandmother that very morning.

He had arrived to visit his father at the clinic just as she was leaving, and she had pounced instantly, commanding him to accompany her to an empty waiting room, obliging him, teeth gritted, to obey.

'Your father tells me you are flying to England today in an attempt to be reconciled with that foolish girl,' she commented acidly, as soon as the door was closed. 'A total waste of your time, my dear Lorenzo. I told my daughter a dozen times that her idea of a marriage between such an ill-assorted pair was wrong-headed and could only end in disaster. And so it has proved. The child has shown herself totally unworthy of the Santangeli family.

'My poor Maria would not pay attention to me, sadly, but you must listen now. Cut your losses and have the marriage dissolved immediately. As I have always suggested, find a good Italian wife who knows what is expected of her and who will devote herself to your comfort and convenience.'

'And naturally, Nonna Teresa, you have a candidate in mind?' His smile was deceptively charming. 'Or even more than one, perhaps? I seem to remember being presented to a positive array of young women whenever I was invited to dine with you.'

'I have given the matter deep thought,' his grandmother conceded graciously. 'And I feel that your eventual choice should be Dorotea Marcona. She is the daughter of an old friend, and a sweet, pious girl who will never give you a moment's uneasiness.'

'Dorotea?' Renzo mused. 'Is she the one who never stops talking, or the one with the squint?'

'A slight cast in one eye,' she reproved. 'Easily corrected by a simple surgical procedure, I understand.'

'For which I should no doubt be expected to pay— the Marcona family having no money.' Renzo shook his head. 'You are the one wasting your time, Nonna Teresa. Marisa is my wife, and I intend that she will remain so.'

'Hardly a wife,' his grandmother said tartly. 'When she lives on the other side of the continent. Your separation threatens to become a public scandal—especially after her mortifying behaviour at the wedding.' She drew her lips into a thin line. 'You cannot have forgotten how she humiliated you?'

'No,' Renzo said quietly. 'I—have not forgotten.'

In fact, thanks to Nonna Teresa, he'd found the memory grating on him all over again—not merely on his way to the airport, but throughout the flight, when it had constantly interfered with his attempts to work. So he'd reached London not in the best of moods, when he should have been conciliatory, only to find his wife missing when he reached the flat.

And when she did return, she was not alone, he thought with cold displeasure. Was with someone other than the Langford man whom he'd come prepared to deal with. Someone, in fact, who should have been history where Marisa was concerned.

And to set the seal on his annoyance, his bride had not been in the least disconcerted, nor shown any sign of guilt over being discovered entertaining a former boyfriend.

But then, attack had always been her favourite form of defence, he recalled grimly, as his mind went back to their wedding day.

He'd always regarded what had happened then as the start of his marital troubles, but now he was not so sure, he thought, twisting round on the sofa to give his unoffending pillow a vicious thump. Hadn't the problems been there from the very beginning? Even on the day when he'd asked Marisa to marry him, and felt the tension emanating from her like a cold hand on his skin, forcing him to realise for the first time just how much forbearance would be required from him in establishing any kind of physical relationship between them.

Nevertheless, the end of the wedding ceremony itself had certainly been the moment that had sounded the death knell of all his good intentions towards his new bride, he thought, his mouth tightening.

He could remember so vividly how she'd looked as she had joined him at the altar of the ancient parish church in Montecalento, almost ethereal in the exquisite drift of white wild silk that had clothed her, and so devastatingly young and lovely that the muscles in his chest had constricted at the sight of her—until he'd seen her pale, strained face, clearly visible under the filmy tulle of her billowing veil. Then that sudden surge of frankly carnal longing had been replaced by compassion, and a renewed determination that he would be patient, give her all the time she needed to accept her new circumstances.

He remembered too how her hand had trembled in his as he'd slid the plain gold wedding band into place, and how there'd been no answering pressure to the tiny comforting squeeze he'd given her fingers.

And how he'd thought at the time, troubled, that it almost seemed as if she was somewhere else—and a long way distant from him.

He'd heard the Bishop give the final blessing, then turned to her, slowly putting the veil back from her face.

She had been looking down, her long lashes curling on her cheeks, her slender body rigid under the fragile delicacy of her gown.

And he'd bent to kiss her quivering mouth, swiftly and very gently, in no more than a token caress, wanting to reassure her by his tender restraint that he would keep his word, that she would have nothing to fear when they were alone together that night.

But before his lips could touch hers Marisa had suddenly looked up at him, her eyes glittering with scorn, and turned her head away so abruptly that his mouth had skidded along her cheekbone to meet with just a mouthful of tulle and few silken strands of perfumed hair.

There had been an audible gasp from the Bishop, and a stir in the mass of the congregation like a wind blowing across barley, telling Renzo quite unequivocally, as he'd straightened, heated colour storming into his face, that his bride's very public rejection of his first kiss as her husband had been missed by no one present. And that she'd quite deliberately made him look a fool.

After which, of course, he'd had to walk the length of the long aisle, with Marisa's hand barely resting on his arm, forcing himself to seem smiling and relaxed, when in fact he had been furiously aware of the shocked and astonished glances being aimed at them from some directions—and the avid enjoyment from others.

Tenderness was a thing of the past, he had vowed angrily. His overriding wish was to be alone somewhere with his bride where he could put her across his knee and administer the spanking of her life.

But instead there had been the ordeal of the wedding breakfast, being held in the warm sunlight of the main square so that the whole town could share in the future Marchese's happiness with his new wife. Where there would be laughter, toasting, and sugared almonds to be handed out, before he and Marisa would be expected to open the dancing.

What would she do then? he had wondered grimly. Push him away? Stamp on his foot? God alone knew.

However, she must have undergone a partial change of heart, because she had gone through the required rituals with apparent docility—although Renzo had surmised bitterly that they must be the only newly-weds in the world to spend the first two hours of their marriage without addressing one word to each other.

It had only been when they were seated stiffly side by side, in the comparative privacy of the limousine returning them to the villa to change for their honeymoon trip, that he'd broken the silence.

'How dared you do such a thing?' His voice was molten steel. 'What possessed you to refuse my kiss—to shame me like that in front of everyone?'

She said huskily, 'But that was exactly why. You've never made any attempt to kiss me before, and, believe me, that's suited me just fine.' She took a breath. 'But now all of a sudden there's an audience present, so you have to play the part of the ardent bridegroom—make the token caring gesture in order to look good in the eyes of your friends and family. So that you might make them think it's a real marriage instead of the payment of a debt—a sordid business deal that neither of us wants.'

She shook her head. 'Well—I won't do that. I won't pretend for the sake of appearances. And you, *signore*,' she added with a little gasp, 'you won't make me.'

There was another silence, then Renzo said icily, 'I trust you have quite finished?' and saw her nod jerkily before she turned away to stare out of the car window.

Only it had not been finished at all, he thought bleakly as he pulled the blanket closer round him and turned awkwardly onto his side. On the contrary, it had been just the beginning of a chain of events from which the repercussions were still impacting on their lives. And God only knew how it might end.

She felt, Marisa thought, as if she'd swallowed a large lump of marble.

Curled into a ball in the middle of the bed, she tugged the coverlet over her head in an effort to shut out the ever-present hum of London traffic through the open window, just as if that was the only reason she couldn't sleep.

Yet who was she trying to fool? she asked herself ironically.

Renzo's unexpected reappearance in her life had set every nerve ending jangling, while her mind was occupied in an endless examination of everything he'd said to her.

Especially his galling assertion that it had been mistakes by them both that had caused the collapse of their marriage.

Because it was his fault—*all* his fault. That was what she'd told herself—the mantra she'd repeated almost obsessively during the endless nightmare of their honeymoon and since. Her determined and in-flexible belief ever since.

Yet now, suddenly, she was not so sure.

She should have let him kiss her at the wedding and she knew it. Had always known it, if she was honest. Realised she should just have stood there and allowed it to happen. And if she hadn't responded—had refused to return the pressure of his lips—her point would have been made, but just between the two of them. No one else would ever have known.

Julia, in particular.

'Are you off your head?' her cousin had said furiously, cornering her in the pretence of straightening her veil. 'My God, he must be blazing. If you know what's good for you tonight you'll forget your little rebellion, lie on your back and pray that he puts you up the stick. Redeem yourself that way—by doing what you've been hired for.'

'Thank you for the unnecessary reminder,' Marisa threw back defiantly and moved away, her half-formed resolve to go to Renzo, to tell him she'd been overcome by nerves and obeyed an impulse that she'd instantly regretted, melting like ice in the hot sunlight.

Neither was her mood improved by their first exchange in the car, nor during the largely silent journey down to their honeymoon destination near Amalfi—the first time, she realised, that she'd been entirely alone with him since he proposed to her. A reflection she found disturbing.

It wasn't the first time he'd ignored her, of course, she thought ruefully, casting a wary glance at his stony profile, but that had been when she was younger, because he'd regarded her as something of a pest. Not because he was angry and humiliated.

And she knew with a kind of detachment that she would have to pay for what she'd done in one way or another.

It occurred to her too that she'd never been his passenger before—another first for her to add to all the others—and as the low, powerful car sped down the *autostrada* under his casually controlled expertise she remembered a jokey magazine article she'd once read, which had suggested a man's sexual performance could often be judged by the way he drove.

She observed the light touch of his lean fingers on the wheel and found herself suddenly wondering how they would feel on her skin, before deciding, with a swift churning sensation in the pit of her stomach as Julia's words came back to haunt her, that from now on she would do better to concentrate firmly on the scenery. However, as the silence between them became increasingly oppressive, she felt that a modest conversational overture might be called for.

She said, 'The villa—is it in Amalfi itself?'

'No, in a village farther along the coast.'

His tone was not particularly inviting, but she persevered.

'And you said it belongs to your godfather?'

'Yes, it is his holiday retreat.'

'It's—kind of him to offer it.'

He gave a faint shrug. 'It is quiet, and overlooks the sea, so he felt it would be a suitably romantic location for a newly married couple to begin their life together.' He added curtly, 'As he was at the wedding, I am sure he now realises his error.'

Marisa subsided, flushing. So much for trying to make conversation, she thought.

She looked down at her slim smooth legs, at the slender pink-tipped feet displayed by the elegant and expensive strappy sandals she was wearing—the same hyacinth-blue as her sleeveless dress.

Apart from having her hair cut, she'd not been a great frequenter of hair and beauty salons in the past, but that had all changed in the last few days, when she'd been taken to Florence and waxed, plucked, manicured and pedicured to within an inch of her life in some pastel, scented torture chamber.

She'd endured the ministrations of various beauticians in a state of mute rebellion, and as perfumed creams and lotions had been applied to the softness of her skin she'd found herself thinking that maybe the old joke about 'Have her stripped, washed and brought to my tent' wasn't so damned funny after all. That there was nothing faintly amusing in finding herself being deliberately prepared for the pleasure of a man.

The beautician had imagined, of course, that she rejoiced in all the intimate preparations because she was in love and wanted to be beautiful for her lover. She'd seen the hastily concealed envy in their faces when they realised the identity of her bridegroom.

What girl, after all, would not want to spend her nights in the arms of Lorenzo Santangeli?

If they only knew, she thought wryly, wondering what other women passed their time in similar salons, being pampered for his delight.

Even that morning two girls had arrived at the villa—one to do her hair, the other her make-up—and she'd been presented with a beauty case containing everything that had been used. Presumably so that she could keep up the good work while she was away, she thought, biting her lip.

Except that it was all a complete waste of time and effort. Renzo had married her by arrangement, not as an object for his romantic desires, but in order to provide himself with a mother for his heir, because she was young, healthy and suitably innocent.

Not the kind of fate she had ever envisaged for herself, she acknowledged with an inward pang. But this was the situation, and she would have to learn to make the best of it—eventually.

And it might indeed have been a step in the right direction if she'd made herself accept that token kiss in church earlier, she thought uneasily. At least they'd have commenced this so-called honeymoon on talking terms. Whereas now...

Even at this late stage, and if they hadn't been on a

motorway, she might actually have been tempted to request him to pull over, so that she could follow her original plan and offer him some kind of apology. Try at least to improve matters between them.

But that clearly wasn't going to happen in the middle of the *autostrada*, and besides, she had a whole month ahead of her in which to make amends—if that was what she wanted, of course, she thought, her hands knotting together in her lap. At the moment she felt too unsettled to decide on any definite course of action.

In addition, Renzo might well have his own ideas on how their marriage should be conducted, she reminded herself dejectedly, stifling a sigh as she risked another wary glance at his unyielding expression.

But no amount of dejection could possibly have survived her first glimpse of the enchanting coastline around Amalfi.

Marisa leaned forward with an involuntary gasp of delight as she saw the first small town, its white buildings gleaming in the late-afternoon sunlight, clinging intrepidly to the precipitous rocky slopes above the restless sea which dashed itself endlessly against them in foam-edged shades of turquoise, azure and emerald.

The road itself, however, was an experience all its own, as it wound recklessly and almost blindly between high cliffs on one side and the toe-curling drop to the sea on the other. The rockface didn't seem very stable either, Marisa thought apprehensively, noting the signs warning of loose boulders, and the protective netting spread along the areas most at risk.

But Renzo seemed totally unconcerned as he skilfully negotiated one breath-stopping bend after another, so she sat back and tried to appear relaxed in her turn. She wasn't terribly successful, to judge by the swift and frankly sardonic glance she encountered from him at one point.

'If it's all the same to you, just keep your eyes on the damned road,' she muttered under her breath.

Yet, if she was honest, her nervousness wasn't entirely due to the vagaries of the *Costiera Amalfitana.* It was perfectly obvious that they would soon arrive at their destination, and she would find herself sharing a roof with him—no longer as his guest, but as his wife.

And that infinitely tricky moment seemed to have come, she thought, her fingers twisting together even more tightly as they turned inland and began to climb a steep narrow road. Marisa glimpsed a scattering of houses ahead of them, but before they were reached Renzo had turned the car between tall wrought-iron gates onto a winding gravel drive which led down to a large, sprawling single-storey house, roofed in faded terracotta, its white walls half-hidden by flowering vines and shrubs.

He said quietly and coldly, as he brought the car to a halt. '*Ecco*, La Villa Santa Caterina. And my godfather's people are waiting to welcome us, so let us observe the conventions and pretend we are glad to be here, if you please.'

Outside the air-conditioned car it was still very warm, but the faint breeze was scented with flowers, and Marisa paused, drawing a deep, grateful breath, before Renzo took her hand, guiding her forward to the beaming trio awaiting them.

'Marisa, this is Massimo, my godfather's major-domo.' He indicated a small thin man in a grey linen jacket and pinstripe trousers. 'Also his wife, Evangelina, who keeps house here and cooks, and Daniella, their daughter, who works as the maid.'

Evangelina must be very good at her job, Marisa thought, as she smiled and uttered a few shy words of greeting in halting Italian, because she was a large, comfortable woman with twinkling eyes, and twice the size of her husband. Daniella too verged towards plump.

Inside the house there were marble floors, walls washed in pastel colours, and the coolness of ceiling fans.

Marisa found herself conducted ceremoniously by Evangelina to a large bedroom at the back of the house. It was mainly occupied by a vast bed, its white coverlet embroidered with golden flowers, heaped with snowy pillows on which tiny sprigs of sweet lavender had been placed.

It was like a stage setting, thought Marisa, aware of a coyly significant glance from Evangelina. But contrary to the good woman's expectations, the leading lady in this particular production would be sleeping there alone tonight, and for the foreseeable future.

The only other pieces of furniture were a long dressing table, with a stool upholstered in gold brocade, and a chaise longue covered in the same material, placed near the sliding glass doors which led onto the verandah.

On the opposite side of the room, a door opened into a bathroom tiled in misty green marble, with a shower that Marisa reckoned was as big as her cousin Julia's box room.

Another door led to a dressing room like a corridor, lined with drawer units and fitted wardrobes, and at the far end this, in turn, gave access to another bedroom of a similar size, furnished in the same way as the first one except that the coverlet was striped in gold and ivory.

Presumably this was the room which Renzo would be using—at least for the time being, she thought, her mouth suddenly dry. And she was relieved to see that it, too, had its own bathroom.

Turning away hurriedly, she managed to smile at Evangelina and tell her that everything was wonderful—magnificent—to the housekeeper's evident gratification.

Back in her own room, she began to open one of her suitcases but was immediately dissuaded by Evangelina, who indicated firmly that this was a job for Daniella, who would be overjoyed to wait upon the bride of Signor Lorenzo.

All this goodwill, Marisa thought with irony, as she followed the housekeeper to the *salotto*, where coffee was waiting. Yet how much of it would survive once it became clear to the household, as it surely would, that the bride of Signor Lorenzo was totally failing to live up to everyone's expectations?

She'd braced herself for another silent interlude, but Renzo was quietly civil, showing her the charming terrace where most of their meals would be taken, and explaining how the rocky local terrain had obliged the large gardens to be built on descending levels, connected by steps and pathways, with a swimming pool and a sunbathing area constructed at the very bottom.

'My godfather says the climb keeps him healthy,' Renzo said, adding with faint amusement, 'His wife has always claimed it is all part of a plot to kill her. But it does not, however, stop her using the pool every day.'

She looked over the balustrade down into the green depths. 'Do you have the same plan, perhaps?' It seemed worth carrying on the mild joke.

'Why, no,' Renzo drawled, his glance travelling over her. 'You, *mia bella*, I intend to keep very much alive.'

I suppose I led with my chin there, thought Marisa, crossly aware she was blushing a little. And if he's going to say things like that, I'd much rather he was silent again.

No one ate early in Italy, and she was used to that, but by the time dinner was eventually served the strain of the day was beginning to tell on her.

She was ruefully aware that she had not done justice to the excellence of Evangelina's cooking, especially the sea bream which had formed the main course, and her lack of appetite was not lost on her companion.

'You are not hungry? Or is there something you would prefer?'

'Oh, no,' she denied hurriedly. 'The fish is wonderful. I'm just very tired—and I think I'm getting a headache,' she added for good measure. 'Perhaps you'd apologise to Evangelina for me—and excuse me.'

'Of course.' He rose politely to his feet. *'Buona notte, mia cara.'*

She walked sedately to the door, trying hard not to appear as if she was running away, but knowing he wouldn't be fooled for a minute. But at least he'd let her go, and what conversation there'd been during the meal had been on general topics, avoiding the personal.

In her bedroom, she saw that the bed had been turned down on both sides, and that one of her trousseau nightgowns, a mere wisp of white crêpe de Chine, had been prettily arranged on the coverlet.

More scene-setting, she thought. But the day's drama was thankfully over.

She had a warm, scented bath, and then changed into the nightgown that Daniella had left for her because there was little to choose between any of them. In fact all her trousseau, she thought, had been chosen with Renzo's tastes in mind rather than hers.

Not that she knew his tastes—or wanted to—she

amended quickly, but this diaphanous cobweb of a thing, with its narrow ribbon steps, would probably be considered to have general masculine appeal.

She climbed into the bed and sank back against the pillows, where the scent of lavender still lingered, aware of an odd sense of melancholy that she could neither dismiss or explain.

Sleep's what I need, she told herself. *Things will seem better in the morning. They always do.*

She was just turning on her side when an unexpected sound caught her attention, and she shot upright again, staring towards the dressing room as its door opened and Renzo came in.

'What are you doing here?' she demanded huskily.

'An odd question, *mia bella*, to put to your husband when he visits your bedroom on your wedding night.'

She sat rigidly against the pillows, watching him approach. He was wearing a black silk robe, but his bare chest, with its dark shadowing of hair, and his bare legs suggested that there was nothing beneath it.

She lifted her chin. 'I—I said I was tired. I thought you accepted that.'

'Also that you had a headache.' He nodded. 'And by now you have probably thought of a dozen other methods to keep me at a distance. I suggest you save them for the future. You will not, however, need them tonight,' he added, seating himself on the edge of the bed.

It was a wide bed, and there was a more than respectable space between them, but in spite of that Marisa still felt that he was too close for comfort. She wanted to move away a little, but knew that he would notice and draw his own conclusions. And she did not wish him to think she was in any way nervous, she thought defensively.

As for what he was wearing—well, she'd seen him in far less in the past, when she'd been swimming or sunbathing in his company, but that, somehow, was a very different matter.

She marshalled her defences. 'You still haven't said why you're here.'

He said, 'I have come to bid you goodnight.'

'You did that downstairs.'

'But I believe that there are things that remain to be said between us.'

He paused. 'We have not begun well, you and I, and these difficulties between us should be settled at once.'

'What—what do you mean?'

He traced the gold thread on the coverlet with a fingertip. 'Earlier today you implied that I had been less than ardent in my wooing of you. But if I stayed aloof it was only because I believed it was what you wanted.'

'And so it was,' she said. 'I said so.'

'Yet if that is true,' he said softly, 'why mention the matter at all?'

She said defiantly, 'I was simply letting you know what a hypocritical farce I find this entire arrangement. And that I won't play games in public just to satisfy some convention.'

'How principled,' he said, and shifted his position, moving deliberately closer to her. 'But we are no longer in public now, *mia cara*. We are in total privacy. So there is no one else to see or care what I ask from you.'

She swallowed. 'You—promised that you— wouldn't ask.' Her voice was thin. 'So I'd really like you to go—please.'

'In a moment,' he said. 'When I have what I came for.'

'I—I don't understand.'

'It is quite simple,' he said. 'I wish to kiss you good-night, Maria Lisa. To take from your lovely mouth what you denied me this morning—nothing more.'

She stared at him. 'You said you'd wait…'

'And I will.' He leaned forward, brushing a strand of hair back from her face. 'But I think—don't you?—that when you come to me as my wife it will be easier for both of us if you have become even a little accustomed to my touch, and learned not to dread being in my arms.'

'What are you saying, *signore*?' Her voice sounded very young and breathless. 'That I'm going to find your kisses so irresistible that I'll want more and more of them? That eventually I'll want you?'

She shook her head. 'That's not going to happen. Because you can dress up what you've done any way you like, but the fact is you bought me. Anything you do to me will be little more than legalised rape.'

There was a terrible silence, then Renzo said, too quietly, too evenly, 'You will never use such a word to me again, Maria Lisa. Do you understand? I told you I would not force myself on you and I meant it. But you would be unwise to try my patience twice in twenty-four hours.'

She threw back her head. 'Your loss of temper doesn't seem much to set against the ruin of my life, Signor Santangeli. Whatever—I have no intention of kissing you. So please leave. Now.'

'And I think not.' Renzo took her by the shoulders, pulling her towards him, his purpose evident in his set face.

'Let me go.' She began to struggle against the strength of the hands that held her, scared now, but still determined. 'I won't do this—I won't.'

She pushed against his chest, fists clenched, her face averted.

'*Mia cara*, this is silly.' He spoke more gently, but there was a note in his voice that was almost amusement. 'Such a fuss about so little. One kiss and I'll go, I swear it.'

'You'll go to hell.' As she tried to wrench herself free one of the ribbon straps on her nightgown suddenly snapped, and the flimsy bodice slipped down, baring one rounded rose-tipped breast.

She froze in horror, and realised that Renzo too was very still, his dark face changing with a new and disturbing intensity as he looked at her. His hand slid slowly down from her shoulder to a more intimate objective, cupping her breast in lean fingers that shook a little. He brushed her nipple softly with the ball of his thumb, and as it hardened beneath his touch she felt sensation scorch through her like a naked flame against her flesh. Frightening her in a way she had never known before.

'No.' Her voice cracked wildly on the word. 'Don't touch me. Oh, God, you *bastard.*'

She flailed out wildly with her fists, and felt the jolt as one of them slammed into his face.

He gave a gasp of pain and reared back away from her, his hand going up to his eye. Then there was another silence.

She thought, the breath catching in her throat, *Oh, God, what have I done? And, even worse, what is he going to do?*

She tried to speak, to say his name—anything. To tell him she hadn't meant to hit him—or at least not as hard.

Only she didn't get the chance. Because he was lifting himself off the bed and striding away from her across the room without looking back. And as Marisa sank back, covering her own face with her hands, she heard first the slam of the dressing room door and then, like an echo, the bang of his own door closing.

And knew with total certainty that for tonight at least he would not be returning.

CHAPTER FIVE

EVEN after all this time Marisa found that the memory still had the power to crucify her.

I'd never behaved like that before in my entire life, she thought, shuddering. *Because I'm really not the violent type—or I thought I wasn't until that moment. Then—pow! Suddenly, the eagle landed. Only it wasn't funny.*

So completely not funny, in fact, that she'd immediately burst into a storm of tears, burying her face in the pillow to muffle the sobs that shook her entire body. Not that he could have heard her, of course. The dressing room and two intervening doors had made sure of that.

But why was I crying? she asked herself, moving restively across the mattress, trying to get comfortable. *After all, it was an appalling thing to do, and I freely admit as much, but it got him out of my bedroom, which was exactly what I wanted to happen.*

And he never came back. Not even after...

She swallowed, closing her eyes, wishing she could blank out all the inner visions that still tormented her. That remained there at the forefront of her mind, harsh and inescapable. Forcing her once again to recall everything that had happened that night—and, even more shamingly, on the day that had followed....

Once she was quite sure that he'd gone, her first priority was to wash the tearstains from her pale face and exchange her torn nightgown for a fresh one—although that, she soon discovered, did nothing to erase the remembered shock of his touch on her bare breast.

So much for his promise to leave her alone until she was ready, she thought, biting her lip savagely.

The way he'd looked at her, the delicate graze of his hand on her flesh, proved how little his word could be trusted.

Yet at the same time it had brought home to her with almost terrifying force how fatally easy it would be to allow her untutored senses to take control, and to forget the real reason—the only reason—they were together.

She'd agreed to this marriage only to repay a mountainous debt and to make life easier for a sick man who'd been good to her. Nothing else.

Lorenzo had accepted the arrangement solely out of duty to his family. And to keep a promise to a dying woman. That was all, too.

'Oh, Godmother,' she whispered under her breath. 'How could you do this to me? To both of us?'

She'd assumed Renzo's offer to postpone the consummation of their marriage was a sign of his basic indifference. Now she didn't now what to think.

Because it seemed that Julia's crude comments about his readiness to take full advantage of the situation might have some basis in truth, after all. That he might indeed find her innocence a novelty after the glamorous, experienced women he was used to, and would, therefore, be able to make the best of a bad job.

'But I can't do that,' she whispered to herself. And as for learning gradually to accustom herself to the idea of intimacy with him, as he'd suggested—well, that would never happen in a million years.

A tiger in the sack, she recalled, wincing. Although she'd tried hard not to consider the implications in Julia's crudity, the way Renzo had touched her had provided her with an unwanted inkling of the kind of demands he might make.

But then she'd known all along that spending her nights with her bridegroom would prove to be a hideous embarrassment at the very least. Or spending some of her nights, she amended hastily. Certainly not all of them. Maybe not very many, and hopefully never the entire night.

Because surely he would soon tire of her sexual naiveté?

In some ways she knew him too well, she thought. In others she didn't know him at all. But on both counts the prospect of sleeping with him scared her half to death.

Not, of course, that sleeping would actually be the problem, she thought, setting her teeth.

She'd tried to play down her fears—telling herself that all he required was a child, a son to inherit the Santangeli name and the power and wealth it represented—and had spent time before the wedding steeling herself to accept that part of their bargain, to endure whatever it took to achieve it, assuring herself that his innate good breeding would ensure that the...the practicalities of the situation would be conducted in a civilised manner.

Only to blow her resolution to the four winds when he'd attempted to kiss her for the first time and she'd panicked. Badly.

She had reason, she told herself defensively. The night of her nineteenth birthday had made her wonder uneasily if Renzo might not want more from her than unwilling submission. And the last half-hour had only confirmed her worst fears—which was why she'd lashed out at him like that.

Her relationship with him had always been a tricky one, she thought unhappily. Leading his own life, he'd figured in her existence, when he chose to appear there, as eternally glamorous and usually aloof. Casually kind to her when it suited him, even occasionally coaching her at tennis and swimming, although never with any great enthusiasm, and almost certainly at his mother's behest—as she'd realised later.

But all that had ended summarily when, longing for

him just once to see her as a woman instead of a child, she'd made a disastrously misguided attempt to emulate one of the girls who'd stayed at the villa as his guest by 'losing' her bikini top when she was alone with him in the swimming pool—only to experience the full force of his icy displeasure.

'If you think to impress me by behaving like a slut, you have misjudged the matter, Maria Lisa.' His words and tone of voice had flayed the skin from her. 'You are too young and too green to be a temptress, my little stork, and you dishonour not only yourself, but my parents' roof with such ridiculous and juvenile antics.' He'd contemptuously tossed the scrap of sodden fabric to her. 'Now, cover yourself and go to your room.'

Overwhelmed by distress and humiliation, she had fled, despising herself for having revealed her fledgling emotions so openly, and agonising over the result.

She had felt only relief when her visits to Tuscany had gone into abeyance, and in time had even been able to reassure herself that any talk about her being Renzo's future bride had been simply sentimental chat between two mothers, and could not, thankfully, be taken seriously.

And if I never see him again, she'd thought defiantly, it will be altogether too soon.

Now, when she looked back, she could candidly admit that she must have been embarrassment on a stick even before the swimming pool incident.

But that being the case, why hadn't he fought tooth and nail not to have her foisted on him as a wife only a few years later?

Surely he must have recognised that there was no chance of their marriage working in any real sense?

On the other hand, perhaps he didn't actually require it to work in that way. Because for him it was simply a means to an end. A business arrangement whereby her body became just another commodity for him to purchase.

Something for his temporary amusement that could be discreetly discarded when its usefulness was finished.

When she'd had his baby.

This was the viewpoint she'd chosen to adopt, and so, in spite of Julia's insinuations, she hadn't really expected him to behave as if—as if he— wanted her...

Or was that just a conditioned reflex? Girl equals bed equals sex? Identity unimportant.

That, she thought with a little sigh, was the likeliest explanation.

For a moment she stood staring at herself in the mirror, studying the shape of her body under the thin fabric of her nightdress. Noticing the length of her legs and the way the shadows in the room starkly reduced the contours of her face, making her features stand out more prominently. Especially her nose...

The stork, she thought painfully, was alive and well

once more. And certainly not likely to be the object of anyone's desire. Renzo's least of all.

She turned away, smothering a sigh, and made her slow, reluctant way back to the bed, lying there shivering in its vastness in spite of the warmth of the night.

Still listening intently, she realised, for the sound of his return, no matter how many times she promised herself that it wasn't going to happen. While at the same time, in her head, the events of the day kept unrolling before her in a seemingly endless loop of error and embarrassment.

It was several hours before she finally dropped into a troubled sleep. And for the first time in years there was no bedside alarm clock to summon her into a new morning, so she woke late to find Daniella at her bedside with a tray of coffee, her dark eyes sparking with ill-concealed interest and excitement as she studied Signor Lorenzo's new bride.

Looking to see how I survived the night, Marisa realised, sitting up self-consciously, aware that her tossing and turning had rumpled the bed sufficiently to make it appear that she hadn't slept alone.

My God, she thought, as she accepted the coffee with a stilted word of thanks. If she only knew…

And silently thanked heaven that she didn't. That no one knew, apart from Renzo and herself, what a total shambles her first twenty-four hours of marriage had been.

Daniella's grasp of English was limited, but Marisa

managed to convince her gently but firmly that she could draw her own bath and choose her own clothing for the day without assistance, uttering a silent sigh of relief when the girl reluctantly withdrew, after informing her that breakfast would be served on the rear terrace.

Because she needed to be alone in order to think.

She'd made a few decisions before she'd eventually allowed herself to sleep, and rather to her surprise they still seemed good in daylight.

The first of them was that this time she must—*must*—apologise to Renzo without delay, and offer him some kind of explanation for her behaviour. She had no other choice.

But that would not be easy, she thought, cautiously sipping the dark, fragrant brew. Because if she simply told him that she'd been too scared to let him kiss her he would almost certainly want to know why.

And she could hardly admit that the angry words she'd hurled at him last night might in fact be only too true. That she'd feared she might indeed find the lure of his mouth on hers hard to resist.

No, she thought forcefully. And no again. That was a confession she dared not make. A painful return to adolescent fantasy land, as unwelcome as it was unexpected. Threatening to make her prey to the kind of dreams and desires she'd thought she'd banished for ever, and which she could not risk again. Not after they'd crashed in ruins the first time.

Oh, God, she thought, swallowing. I'm going to have to be so careful. I need to make him believe it was just a serious fit of bridal nerves.

From which I've now recovered...

Because that was important, she told herself, when considering the next huge obstacle she had to overcome. Which was, of course, the inevitable and unavoidable establishment of their marriage on as normal a footing as it was possible to achieve—given the circumstances.

She replaced her empty cup on the bedside table and drew up her knees, wrapping her arms around them. Frowning as she wondered how she could possibly tell him that she was now prepared to fulfil her side of their arrangement. While making it quite clear, at the same time, that she intended to regard any physical contact between them as solely part of a business deal and certainly not the beginning of any kind of—relationship.

He didn't require her for that, anyway, she thought. According to Julia his needs in that respect were already well catered for by—what was her name? Ah, yes, Lucia, she recalled stonily. Lucia Gallo.

And throwing aside the covers, she got out of bed and prepared to face the day.

She hadn't taken a great deal of interest in the purchase of her trousseau, except to veto her cousin's more elaborate choice of evening dresses. But here she was, on the first morning of her marriage, with a tricky confrontation ahead of her, so choosing something to wear from the array that Daniella had unpacked and hung in one of the dressing room closets, suddenly seemed to acquire an additional importance.

She finally decided on one of her simplest outfits, a square-necked, full-skirted dress in pale yellow cotton. She brushed her light brown hair into its usual style, curving softly on to her shoulders, and added a coating of mascara to her lashes, a coral-based colour to her lips.

Then, slipping on low-heeled tan leather sandals, she left the bedroom and went in reluctant search of Lorenzo.

She'd assumed he would be at the breakfast table, but when she walked out into the sunshine she saw that only a single place was set in the vine-shaded pergola.

She turned to Massimo in faint surprise. 'The *signore* has eaten already?'

'*Si, signora*. Early. Very early. He say you are not to be disturbed.' He paused, his face lugubrious. 'And then he goes out in the car. Maybe to see a doctor—for his accident.'

'Accident?' Marisa repeated uneasily.

Evangelina came surging out to join them, bearing a fresh pot of coffee and a plate of sweet rolls to add to the platter of ham and cheese already on the table.

'*Si, signora*,' she said. 'Last night, in the dark, Signor Lorenzo he walk into door.' Her reproachful glance suggested that the *signore* should have been safely in bed, engrossed with his new bride, rather than wandering around bumping into the fixtures and fittings.

Marisa felt her colour rise. 'Oh, that,' she said, trying to sound nonchalant. 'Surely it isn't that bad?'

Pursed lips and shrugs invited her to think again, and her heart sank like a stone as it occurred to her that Renzo might not be feeling particularly receptive to any overtures this morning, and that her apology might have to be extremely humble indeed if it was to cut any ice with him.

Which was not altogether what she'd planned.

She hung around the terrace most of the morning, waiting with trepidation for his return. And waiting...

Until Massimo came, clearly bewildered, to relay the *signore*'s telephone message that he would be lunching elsewhere.

Marisa, managing to hide her relief, murmured *'Che peccato,'* and set herself to the task of persuading Massimo that it was far too hot for the midday banquet Evangelina seemed to be planning and that, as she would be eating alone, clear soup and a vegetable risotto would be quite enough.

She still wasn't very hungry, but starving herself would do no good, so she did her best with the food, guessing that any lack of appetite would be ascribed to the fact that she was pining for Lorenzo.

She was already aware that glances were being exchanged over her head in concern for this new wife left to her own devices so soon after her bridal night.

If Renzo continued his absence they might start putting two and two together and making all kinds of numbers, she thought without pleasure.

Her meal finished, she rested for a while in her room with the shutters drawn, but she soon accepted that she was far too jittery to relax, so she changed into a black bikini, topping it with a pretty black and white voile overshirt, and went back into the sunshine to find the swimming pool.

As Renzo had indicated, it was quite a descent through tier upon tier of blossom-filled terraces. It was like climbing down into a vast bowl of flowers, Marisa thought, with the oval pool, a living aquamarine, at its base. The sun terrace surrounding the water was tiled in a mosaic pattern of ivory and gold, and sunbeds had been placed in readiness, cushioned in turquoise, each with its matching parasol.

At one end of the pool there was a small hexagonal pavilion, painted white, containing towels, together with extra cushions and a shelf holding an extensive range of sun protection products. It also contained a refrigerator stocked with bottled water and soft drinks.

The air was very still, and filled with the scent of the encircling flowers. The only sounds were the soft drone of bees searching for pollen and, farther away, the whisper of the sea.

Marisa took a deep breath. If she'd simply been visiting on holiday, by herself, she'd have thought she was in paradise. As it was…

But she wouldn't think about that now, she told herself firmly. For the present she was alone, and she would make the most of it. Even if it was only the calm before an almost inevitable storm.

She slipped off her shirt and walked to the side of the pool. She sat on the edge for a moment, testing the temperature of the water with a cautious foot, then slid in, gasping with pleasure as the exquisite coolness received her heated body.

She began to swim steadily and without haste, completing one length of the pool, then another, and a third, feeling relaxed for the first time in days.

Out of the water, and dried off, she was careful to apply a high-factor lotion to her exposed skin before stretching out to sunbathe.

Allowing herself to burn to a frazzle might be an effective way of postponing the inevitable, she thought ruefully, but it wouldn't do much to advance the cause of marital harmony. And she couldn't afford to let matters deteriorate any further—not now she'd made up her mind to yield herself to him.

She capped the bottle and lay back on the padded cushions of her shaded lounger, closing her eyes and letting her thoughts drift.

Dinner tonight, she supposed, would probably be the best time to tell him of her decision—and then she might well drink herself into oblivion for the first time in her life, which was not something she'd ever contemplated, or a prospect she particularly relished.

It was just a question of doing whatever was necessary to get her through this phase in her life relatively unscathed, she thought unhappily, and alcohol was the only available anaesthetic.

It occurred to her that Renzo would probably know exactly why she was drinking as if tomorrow had been cancelled, but why would he care as long as he got what he wanted? she asked herself defiantly.

Anyway, she'd deal with that when the time came, and in the meantime she should stop brooding and turn her thoughts to something else entirely.

She ought to have brought something to read, she told herself ruefully. But when she'd mentioned packing some books into her honeymoon luggage Julia had stared at her as if she was insane, then told her acidly that Renzo would make sure she had far better things to do with her time.

Which brought her right back to square one again, she thought with a sigh, sitting up and reaching for her shirt.

She'd noticed some magazines yesterday in the *salotto*, and although they seemed exclusively to feature high fashion and interior design, they'd at least be a diversion.

Also they were in Italian, and Zio Guillermo had suggested kindly, but with a certain firmness too, that it would be good for her to start improving her language skills as soon as possible. So she could kill two birds with one stone.

Because of the heat, she deliberately took the climb

up to the terrace very easily, pausing frequently to stand in the shade, and look back over the view.

But as she reached the top of the last flight of steps she halted abruptly, her heart thumping out a warning tattoo against her ribcage.

Because Renzo was there, sitting at the table, his feet up on an adjacent chair, reading a newspaper, a glass of wine beside him. He was wearing brief white shorts, a pair of espadrilles and sunglasses. The rest of him was tanned skin.

There was no way to avoid him, of course, Marisa realised uneasily, because this was the only route to the house. She just wished she was wearing more clothes. Or that he was.

It was all too horribly reminiscent of the last time he'd seen her in a bikini, when she'd given way to an impulse she'd hardly understood and been left to weep at her own humiliation.

She swallowed. But that had been years ago, and she wasn't a child any longer—as he'd demonstrated last night.

And now there were things which had to be said, which couldn't be put off any longer. Three birds, she thought, for the price of two. And bit her lip.

As she stood, hesitating, Renzo glanced up and saw her. Immediately he put his paper aside and got politely to his feet. *'Buon pomeriggio.'* His greeting was unsmiling.

'Good afternoon,' she returned, dry-mouthed. *In*

some odd way, he seemed taller than ever. 'I—I was hoping you'd be back.'

He said expressionlessly, 'I am flattered.'

His tone suggested the opposite, but Marisa ploughed on, trying to look anywhere but directly at him.

'Evangelina said you might need medical treatment. I—I was—concerned.'

'In case I had been blinded?' he questioned with faint derision. He shook his head. 'Evangelina exaggerates. As you see, no doctor was necessary,' he added, removing his dark glasses.

She had to look at him then, staring with horror at the dark bruising at the corner of his eye. It was even worse than she'd expected.

She said huskily, 'I—I'm truly sorry. Please believe that I didn't mean to do it—that it was a total accident.'

He shrugged. 'Then God help me if you ever intend to do it.'

Colour rose in her face. She said, 'I never would. I—I was startled, that's all.' She spread her hands defensively. 'All this—the strain of these last weeks—the wedding—it hasn't been easy for me.'

'And therefore my quite unreasonable wish to kiss you goodnight was the final straw?' he said softly. 'Is that what you are saying?'

She bit her lip. 'Yes—perhaps.' She looked down at the black and white marble tiles at her feet. 'Although I realise it's no excuse.'

'At least we agree on something.'

He was not making this very easy for her, she thought. But then why should he? He was the one with the black eye.

'Also,' she went on, 'I have to thank you for pretending that you walked into a door.'

'It is the usual excuse, I believe,' he said crisply. *'Inoltre*, I felt the truth would hardly be to the credit of either of us.' His mouth twisted. 'And Evangelina would have been most distressed. She is a romantic creature.'

She did not meet his gaze. 'Then we must already be a terrible disappointment to her.'

'No doubt,' he said. 'But we must all learn to live with our various disillusionments.' He shrugged again. 'And for some time to come, it seems, to judge by last night.'

The moment of truth had arrived. Earlier than she'd planned, but a few hours couldn't really matter. Anyway, there was no turning back now, she thought, taking a deep breath. But her voice faltered a little just the same. 'Well—perhaps not.'

There was an odd silence, then Renzo said slowly, 'Why, Maria Lisa, are you saying you want me to make love to you?'

She realised that he was looking at her, studying her, allowing his eyes to travel slowly down her half-naked body. Thought again of a time when she would have responded with eager joy to the caress of his gaze, and how her pathetic attempt to lure him had met with rejection instead.

A small, cold stone seemed to settle in the middle of her chest.

She said, lifting her chin, 'Shall we save the pretence for the staff, *signore*? You don't want me any more than I want you. Julia told me you already have this Lucia Gallo in your life, so we both know exactly why we're here, and what's expected of us, and it has nothing to do with love.'

She stared rigidly past him. 'You said last night that you wanted me not to—not to dread being with you, but that's not going to happen. It—can't. Because, however long you wait, I'm never going to be—ready in the way you wish.'

He was utterly still, she realised, and completely silent. In fact, she could have been addressing a statue. A man of bronze.

Oh, God, she thought. This would have been so much less complicated over dinner. And she wasn't explaining it all in the way she'd rehearsed down at the pool either. In fact, she seemed to be saying all kinds of things she hadn't intended. But she'd started, and she had to go stumbling on. She had no choice now.

'You bought me for a purpose.' Her voice quivered a little. 'So you're entitled to use me—in that way. I— I realise that, and I accepted it when I agreed to marry you. Truly I did. I also accept that you were trying to be kind when you said you'd be patient and—and wait in order to make…sex with you…easier for me. Except, it hasn't worked. Because waiting has just made everything a hundred times worse. It's like this huge black cloud hanging over me—a sentence that's been passed but not carried out.'

She swallowed. 'It's been this way ever since we became engaged, and I can't bear it any longer. So I'd prefer it—over and done with, and as soon as possible.'

She slid a glance at him, and for a brief instant she had the strangest impression that it wasn't only the corner of his eye but his entire face that was bruised.

Some trick of the light, she thought, her throat closing as she hurried on with a kind of desperation.

'So I need to tell you that it's all right—for you to come to my room tonight. I'll do whatever you want, and—I—I promise that I won't fight you this time.' And stopped, at last, with a little nervous gasp.

The silence and stillness remained, but the quality of it seemed to have changed in some subtle way she did not understand.

But all the same it worried her, and she needed it to be broken. To obtain some reaction from him.

She drew a breath. 'Perhaps I haven't explained properly...'

'*Al contrario*, you have been more than clear, *signora*.' His voice reached her at last, cool and level. 'Even eloquent. My congratulations. I am only sorry that my attempt at behaving towards you with consideration has failed so badly. Forgive me, please, and believe I did not intend to cause you stress by delaying the consummation of our marriage.

However, that can soon be put right. And we do not have to wait until tonight.'

Two long strides brought him to her. He picked her up in his arms and carried her towards the open French windows of the *salotto*.

She said, in a voice she did not recognise. 'Renzo—what are you doing?' She began to struggle. 'Put me down—do you hear? Put me down at once.'

'I intend to.' He crossed the room to the empty fireplace, setting her down on the enormous fur rug that fronted it and kneeling over her. He said softly, 'You said you would not fight me, Marisa. I recommend that you keep your promise.'

She looked up at him—at the livid bruising and the hard set of his mouth. At the cold purpose in his eyes.

'Oh, God, no.' Her voice cracked. 'Not like this—please.'

'Do not distress yourself.' His voice was harsh. 'Your ordeal will be brief—far more so than it would have been tonight. And that is my promise to you.'

He reached down almost negligently, stripping her of the bottom half of her bikini and tossing it aside, before unzipping his shorts.

He did not hold her down, nor use any kind of force. Shocked as she was, she could recognise that. But then he did not have to, she thought numbly, because she'd told him that she wouldn't resist.

And he was, quite literally, taking her at her word.

Nor did he attempt to kiss her. And the hand that parted her thighs was brisk rather than caressing.

She tried to say no again, because every untried female instinct she possessed was screaming that it should not be like this.

That, whatever she'd said, this wasn't what she'd intended. That she'd been nervous and muddled it all. And somehow she had to let him know this, and ask him, in spite of everything, to be kind.

But no sound came from her dry, paralysed throat, and anyway it was all too late—because Renzo was already guiding himself slowly into her, pausing to give her bewildered face a swift glance, then taking total possession of her stunned body with one long, controlled thrust.

Arching himself above her, his weight on his arms, his clenched fists buried in the softness of the rug on either side of her, he began to move, strongly and rhythmically.

Marisa had braced herself instinctively against the onset of a pain she'd imagined would be inevitable, even if she'd been taken with any kind of tenderness.

But if there'd been any discomfort it had been so slight and so fleeting that she'd barely registered the fact.

It was the astonishing sensation of his body sheathed in hers that was totally controlling her awareness. The amazing reality of all that potent, silken hardness, driving ever more deeply into her aroused and yielding heat, slowly at first, then much faster, that was sending her mind suddenly into free fall. Alerting her to possibilities she had not known existed. Offering her something almost akin to—hope.

And then, with equal suddenness, it was over. She heard Renzo cry out hoarsely, almost achingly, and felt his body shuddering into hers in one scalding spasm after another.

For what seemed an eternity he remained poised above her, his breathing ragged as he fought to regain his control. Then he lifted himself out of her, away from her, dragging his clothing back into place with frankly unsteady hands before getting to his feet and looking down at her, his dark face expressionless.

'So, *signora*.' His voice was quiet, almost courteous. 'You have nothing more to fear. Our distasteful duty has at last been done, and I trust without too much inconvenience to you.'

He paused, adding more harshly, 'Let us also hope that it has achieved its purpose, and that you are never forced to suffer my attentions again. And that I am not made to endure any further outrage to my own feelings.'

He walked to the door without sparing her one backward glance. Leaving her where she was lying, shaken, but in some strange way feeling almost— bereft without him.

And at that moment, when it was so very much too late, she heard herself whisper his name.

CHAPTER SIX

EVEN now Marisa could remember with total clarity that she hadn't wanted to move.

That it had seemed somehow so much easier to remain where she was, like a small animal cowering in long grass, shivering with resentment, shame and—yes—misery too, than to pull herself together and restore some kind of basic decency to her appearance as she tried to come to terms with what had just happened.

Eventually the fear of being found by one of the staff had forced her to struggle back into her bikini briefs and, huddling her crumpled shirt defensively around her, make her way to her room.

There, she'd stripped completely, before standing under a shower that had been almost too hot to be bearable. As if that could in any way erase the events of the past half-hour.

How could he? she'd asked herself wretchedly as the water had pounded its way over her body. *Oh, God, how could he treat me like that—as if I had no feelings—as if I hardly existed for him?*

Well, I know the answer to that now, Marisa thought, turning over in her search for a cool spot on her pillow. *If I'm honest, I probably knew it then too, but couldn't let myself admit it.*

It happened because that's what I asked for. Because I added insult to the injury I'd already inflicted by telling him to his face that he didn't matter. That sex with him would only ever be a 'distasteful duty'—the words he threw at me afterwards.

She'd sensed the anger in him, like a damped-down fire that could rage out of control at any moment, in the way he'd barely touched her. In the way that the love-making he'd offered her only moments before had been transformed into a brief, soulless act accomplished with stark and icy efficiency. And perhaps most of all in his subsequent dismissal of her before he walked away.

Yet, anger had not made him brutal, she reflected broodingly. He had not behaved well, perhaps. After all, she had still been his new bride, and a virgin, but he had not forced her—merely used her confused and unwilling assent against her. And he most certainly hadn't hurt her.

Or not physically, at least.

Which made it difficult to blame or hate him as much as she wanted to do, she realised, aggrieved.

An important stone that would for ever be missing from the wall of indifference she'd deliberately constructed between them.

And it was a wall that she was determined to maintain

at all costs, Marisa told herself, now that Renzo had so unexpectedly come back into her life, it seemed with every intention of remaining there, totally regardless of her own wishes.

Which surely constituted just cause for resentment, however you looked at it?

Suddenly restive, she pushed the coverlet aside and got out of bed, moving soundlessly to the small easy chair by the window.

If ever she'd needed a good night's sleep to ensure that she was fresh, with all her wits about her for the morning, it was now. And it just wasn't going to happen—thanks to the man occupying her living room sofa and the memories his arrival had forced back into her consciousness.

Memories of leaning slumped against the shower's tiled wall, a hand pressed against her abdomen as she realised it would be nearly three weeks before she knew for certain whether Renzo's 'purpose', as he'd so bleakly expressed it, had been achieved, and his child was growing in her body.

Of trying desperately to formulate some credible excuse to avoid having to face him at dinner in a few hours' time—or ever again, for that matter—and knowing there was none. She would have to pretend that she didn't care how he'd treated her. That she'd neither anticipated nor wanted anything more from him, and was simply thankful that the matter had been dealt with and need not be referred to again.

Of eventually dressing in a pretty swirl of turquoise silk—not white, because it was no longer appropriate, and not black because it might suggest she was in some kind of mourning—and joining him with an assumption of calmness in the *salotto*.

Of accepting his coolly civil offer of a drink with equal politeness, realising he had no more wish to speak of the afternoon's events than she did. And then of sitting opposite him in silence, during an interminable meal.

A pattern, she had soon discovered, that would be repeated each evening.

Not that he'd planned to spend time with her during the day either, as she had found out when she joined him for breakfast the following morning, at his request, conveyed by Daniella.

'This is a very beautiful part of the world, Marisa, and you will no doubt wish to go sightseeing—to explore Amalfi itself, of course, and then discover the delights of Ravello and Positano.'

Was he offering to escort her? she wondered in sudden alarm, her lips already parting to deny, mendaciously, that she had any such ambition. To say she was quite content to stay within the precincts of the villa while he went off to Ravello, or wherever, and stayed there.

But before she could speak, he added smoothly, 'I have therefore arranged to have a car placed at your disposal. The driver's name is Paolo. He is a cousin of Evangelina and completely reliable. He will make himself available each day to drive you anywhere you want to go.'

So I don't have to...

The unspoken words seemed to hover in the air between them.

'I see.' She should have been dancing with relief. Instead, she felt oddly—blank. She hesitated. 'That's—very kind of you.'

He shrugged. 'It's nothing.'

And that she could believe, she thought bleakly. It was his way of dealing with an awkward and disagreeable situation—by simply ridding himself of the source of annoyance.

After all, he'd done it not that long ago—with Alan.

Renzo paused too. He went on more slowly, 'I have also ordered a box of books to be delivered here for you—a selection from the bestseller lists in Britain and America. I recall you used to like thrillers, but perhaps your tastes have changed?'

Marisa found she was biting her lip—hard.

'No,' she said. 'Not really. And I'm very grateful.' Adding stiffly, *'Grazie.'*

'Prego.' His mouth curled slightly. 'After all, *mia bella*, I would not wish you to be bored.'

A comment, she thought stonily, that removed any further need for appreciation on her part.

For the next few days it suited her to play the tourist—if only because it got her away from the villa and Renzo's chillingly aloof courtesy. To her endless embarrassment he continued to treat her with quite astonishing generosity, and as a result she found herself in possession of more money in cash than she'd ever dreamed of in her life, plus a selection of credit cards with no apparent upper limit.

She'd often wondered what it might be like to have access to unrestricted spending, only to find there was very little she actually wanted to buy.

Maybe I'm not the type to shop till I drop, she thought, sighing. *What a waste.*

But she did make one important purchase. In Positano she bought herself three *maillots*—one in black, another in a deep olive-green, and the third in dark red—to wear for her solitary late-afternoon swim, and to replace the bikinis she never wanted to see again, let alone wear.

In Amalfi she visited an outlet selling the handmade paper for which the region was famous, and dutifully bought some to send back to England to Julia and Harry. She also sent her cousin a postcard, with some deliberately neutral comments on the weather and scenery. After all, she thought wryly, she could hardly write *Having a wonderful time.*

She was particularly enchanted by Ravello, its narrow streets seemingly caught in a medieval time warp, and thought wistfully how much she would like to attend one of the open-air concerts held in the moonlit splendour of the gardens at the Villa Rufulo.

But she acknowledged with a sigh, it was hardly the kind of event she could attend alone, without inviting even more speculation than already existed.

Paolo was a pleasant, middle-aged man who spoke good English and was eager to guide her round his amazing native landscape and share his extensive knowledge of its history. But Marisa was conscious that, like the staff at the villa, he was bemused at this bride who seemed never to be in her husband's company, and she was growing tired of being asked if the *signore* was quite well.

Eventually she decided she had visited enough churches, admired enough Renaissance artefacts, and gaped at sufficient pictures. Also, she felt disinclined to give any more assurances about Renzo's health—especially as the bruise on his eye was fading at last.

Her main danger was in eating far too many of the delicious almond and lemon cakes served in the cafés in Amalfi's Piazza del Duomo, as she sat at a table in the sunlight and watched the crowds as they milled about in the ancient square.

So many families strolling with children. So very many couples, too, meeting with smiling eyes, a touch of hands, an embrace. No one, she thought, had ever greeted her like that, as if she was their whole world. Not even Alan. But their relationship hadn't had a chance, being over almost as soon as it had begun.

And then, in her mind, she saw a sudden image of Renzo, standing at the altar only a week before, as if transfixed, an expression that was almost wonder on his dark face as she walked towards him.

And what on earth had made her think of *that*? she thought, startled, as she finished her coffee and signalled for the bill.

Not that it meant anything—except that the sight of her had probably brought it home to him that his head was now firmly in the noose.

All the same, the buzz of talk and laughter in the air around her only served to emphasise her own sense of isolation.

She thought, with a pang, *I have no one. Unless, of course…* And her hand strayed almost unconsciously to the flatness of her stomach.

The next morning, when Evangelina enquired at what hour the *signora* would require Paolo to call for her, Marisa said politely that she did not wish to do any more sightseeing for a while.

'Ah.' Something like hope dawned in the plump face. 'No doubt you will be joining the *signore* by the pool?'

'No,' Marisa returned coolly. 'I thought I would go up to the village for a stroll.'

'The village is small,' said Evangelina. 'It has little to see, *signora*. Better to stay here and relax.' She gave a winning smile. 'Is quiet by the pool. No disturb there.'

In other words, Marisa thought, caught between annoyance and a kind of reluctant amusement, no one would go blundering down there in case the *signore* decided to take full advantage of his wife's company by enjoying his marital rights in such secluded and romantic surroundings.

She shrugged. 'I'll swim later, as usual,' she said casually. 'After I've been for my walk.' And she turned away, pretending not to notice the housekeeper's disappointment.

Fifteen minutes later, trim in a pair of white cut-offs topped by a silky russet tee shirt, with her pretty straw bag slung across her shoulder, Marisa passed through Villa Santa Caterina's wide gateway and set off up the hill.

Evangelina, she soon discovered, had been perfectly correct in her assessment. The village *was* small, and no tourist trap, its main street lined with houses shuttered against the morning sun, interspersed with a few shops providing life's practicalities, among them a café with two tables outside under an awning.

Maybe on the way back she'd stop there for a while and have a cold drink. Enjoy the shade. Read some of the book she'd brought with her. Anything to delay the moment when she would have to return to Villa Santa Caterina and the probability of Evangelina's further attempts to throw her into Renzo's arms.

At the same time she became aware that every few yards, between the houses and their neat gardens, she could catch a glimpse of the sparkling azure that was the sea.

The view from the villa garden was spectacular

enough, she thought, but up here it would be magical, and in her bag she'd also brought the small sketching block and pencils that she'd acquired on yesterday's trip to Amalfi.

She was standing, craning her neck at one point, when she realised the lady of the house in question had emerged and was watching her.

Marisa stepped back, flushing. *'Perdono,'* she apologised awkwardly. 'I was looking at the view— *il bel mare,'* she added for good measure.

Immediately the other's face broke into a beaming smile. *'Si—si,'* she nodded vigorously. She marched over to Marisa and took her arm, propelling her up the village street while chattering at a great and largely incomprehensible rate—apart from the words *'una vista fantastica'*, which pretty much explained themselves.

At the end of the street the houses stopped and a high wall began, which effectively blocked everything. Marisa's self-appointed guide halted, pointing at it.

'Casa Adriana,' she announced. *'Che bella vista.'* She kissed her fingertips as she urged Marisa forward, adding with a gusty sigh, *'Che tragedia.'*

A fantastic view, I can handle, Marisa thought as she moved off obediently. But do I really need a tragedy to go with it?

However, a glance over her shoulder showed that her new friend was still watching and smiling, so she gave a slight wave in return and trudged on.

As she got closer she saw that the wall's white paintwork was dingy and peeling, and that the actual structure was crumbling in places, indicating that some serious attention was needed.

It also seemed to go on for ever, but eventually she realised she was approaching a narrow, rusting wrought-iron gate, and that this was standing ajar in a kind of mute invitation.

Beyond it, a weed-infested gravel path wound its way between a mass of rioting bushes and shrubs, and at its end, beckoning like a siren, was the glitter of blue that announced the promised view.

The breath caught in Marisa's throat, and she pushed the gate wider so that she could walk through. She'd expected an outraged squeal from the ancient metal hinges, but there wasn't a sound. Someone, she saw, had clearly been busy with an oil can.

This is what happens in late night thrillers on television, she told herself. *And I'm always the one with her hands over her face, screaming* Don't do it! *So it will serve me right if that gate swings shut behind me and traps me in here with some nameless horror lurking in the undergrowth.*

But the gate, fortunately, displayed no desire to move, and the nameless horror probably had business elsewhere, so she walked briskly forward, avoiding the overhanging shrubs and bushes with their pollen-heavy blossoms that tried to impede her way.

There was a scent of jasmine in the air, and there

were roses too, crowding everywhere in a rampant glory of pink, white and yellow. Marisa was no expert—her parents' garden had been little more than a grass patch, while Julia had opted for a courtyard with designer tubs—but from her vacations in Tuscany she recognised oleanders mingling with masses of asters, pelargoniums, and clumps of tall graceful daisies, all wildly out of control.

Halfway down, the path forked abruptly to the right, and there, half-eclipsed by the bougainvillaea climbing all over it, was all that remained of a once pretty house. Its walls were still standing, but even from a distance Marisa could see that many of the roof tiles were missing, and that behind the screen of pink and purple flowers shutters were hanging loose from broken windows.

But there'd been attempts elsewhere to restore order. The grass had been cut in places, and over-intrusive branches cut down and stacked, presumably for burning.

In the centre of one cleared patch stood a fountain, where a naked nymph on tiptoe sadly tilted an urn which had not flowed with water for a very long time.

And straight ahead, at the end of the path, a lemon tree heavy with fruit stood like a sentinel, watching by the low wall that overlooked the bay.

Rather too low a wall, Marisa thought, when she took a wary peep over its edge and discovered a stomach-churning drop down the sheer and rocky cliff to the tumbling sea far below.

She stepped back hastily, and found herself colliding with an ancient wooden seat, which had been placed at a safe distance in the shade of the tree, suggesting that the garden's owner might not have had much of a head for heights either.

That was probably the tragedy that her friend in the village had mentioned, she thought. An inadvertent stumble after too much *limoncello* by some unlucky soul, and a headlong dive into eternity.

She seated herself gingerly, wondering if the bench was still capable of bearing even her slight weight, but there was no imminent sign of collapse, so she allowed herself to lean back and take her first proper look at the panorama laid out in front of her.

One glance told her that 'fantastic' was indeed the word, and she silently blessed the woman who'd sent her here.

Over to her left she could see the cream, gold and terracotta of Amalfi town, looking as if it had grown like some sprawling rock plant out of the tall cliffs that sheltered it. The towering stone facades themselves gleamed like silver and amethyst in the morning sun under a dark green canopy of cypresses. And below the town the deep cerulean sea turned to jade and turquoise edged with foam as it spilled itself endlessly on the shingle shore.

She could even see the rooftop swimming pools of the hotels overlooking the port, and the sturdy outline of the medieval watchtower, which no longer scanned

the horizon for pirates or enemies from neighbouring city states, but served food in its elegant restaurant instead. Beyond it lay Ravello, and if she turned
to glance the other way she could see the dizzying
tumble of Positano, and in the far distance a smudge
that might even be Capri.

The horizon was barely visible, sky and sea merg-
ing seamlessly in an azure blur.

It was also very quiet. The sound of traffic along
the ribbon of coast road was barely audible at this
distance, and for the first time in weeks Marisa felt
the tension within her—like the heaviness of unshed
tears—beginning to ease, and something like peace
take its place.

So good, she thought. So good to be truly alone and
leave behind the pressure of other people's expectations. To be free of the necessity of changing into yet
another charming and expensive dress just to make occasional and stilted conversation across a dinner table
with a young man whose smile never reached his eyes.

To be, just for a while, Marisa Brendon again
and nothing more, with no apology for a marriage
to haunt her.

She looked down at her hand, then slowly slid off
her wedding ring, and buried it deep in her pocket.

There, she thought. Now I can pretend that I'm
simply here on vacation, with my whole life ahead of
me, free to enjoy no one's company but my own.

Only to hear from behind her a small, mild cough

which announced that she was not alone after all. That someone else was there, sharing her supposed solitude.

Startled, she jumped to her feet and turned, to find herself confronted by a small woman with rimless glasses and wisps of grey hair escaping from under a floppy linen sun hat. Her khaki trousers and shirt were smeared with earth and green stains, and she carried a small pair of pruning shears in one hand and a flat wicker basket full of trimmings in the other.

Oh, God, Marisa thought, embarrassed colour flooding her face. *That house can't be as derelict as I thought.*

Aloud, she said, in halting and woefully incorrect Italian, 'Please forgive me. I was not told that anyone lived here. I will leave at once.'

The newcomer's brows lifted. 'Another Englishwoman,' said a gentle voice. 'How very nice. And I'm afraid we're both trespassers, my dear. I also came here one day to look at the view, but I saw a potentially beautiful space going to rack and ruin and I couldn't resist the challenge. No one has ever objected,' she added. 'Probably because they think I'm mad to try.'

Her smile was kind. 'So please don't run away on my account. And I'm sorry if I startled you. You were a shock to me too, appearing so quietly. For a moment I thought Adriana had returned, and then I realised you were totally twenty-first century. Quite a relief, I have to say.'

She tugged off her thick gardening gloves and held out her hand. 'I'm Dorothy Morton.'

'Marisa Brendon.' *Well, I've done it now,* Marisa thought as she returned the smile and the handshake. *Crossed my own small Rubicon back to being single again.*

'Marisa,' the older woman repeated thoughtfully. 'Such a charming name. And Italian too, I believe?'

'After my late godmother.'

'Ah,' said Mrs Morton. 'And did she live locally? Are you familiar with the area?'

Marisa shook her head. 'No, this is my first visit.' *And almost certainly my last.* 'I'm staying with—some people.'

'My husband and I were fortunate enough to be able to retire here.' Mrs Morton looked out at the bay with an expression of utter contentment. 'We have an apartment nearby, but it only has a balcony, and I do miss my gardening. So I come here most days and do what I can.' She sighed. 'But as you see, it's an uphill struggle.'

'It must be tiring too.' Marisa gestured towards the bench. 'Shall we sit down—if you have time?'

'My time is very much my own.' Mrs Morton took a seat at the other end of the bench. 'I have a most understanding husband.'

'That's—lovely for you.' Marisa was suddenly conscious of the ring buried in her pocket. She added hurriedly, 'But why has the garden been allowed to get into such a state?' She glanced around her. 'Doesn't the owner—this Adriana—care?'

'I think she would care very much if she was alive to see it, but she died a long time ago—over fifty years, I gather—and ownership of the property is no longer established.'

'She didn't have an heir?' Marisa asked with a certain constraint. Another topic, she thought, she'd have preferred to avoid.

'She and her husband were still newlyweds,' Mrs Morton explained. 'According to the local stories they made wills leaving everything to each other. And when he pre-deceased her she refused to make another.'

She shrugged. 'Relatives on both sides have made legal claims to the estate over the years, but I suspect that most of them have died too by now, so the whole thing is in abeyance.'

'Oh.' Marisa drew a deep breath. 'So that's the tragedy. This wonderful place just left to—moulder away.' She shook her head. 'But why on earth didn't this Adriana change her will?'

'Oh, that's quite simple,' Mrs Morton said quietly. 'You see, she never actually believed that her husband was dead.'

Marisa frowned. 'But surely there must have been a death certificate at some point?' she objected.

'Under normal circumstances,' the other woman said. 'But sadly there was no real proof of death. Filippo Barzoni was sailing back from Ischia—he was a keen and experienced sailor, and had made the trip many times before—when a sudden violent squall blew up. Neither he nor his boat were ever seen again.

'Some wreckage was washed up near Sorrento, but it was considered inconclusive as the storm had produced other casualties. However, no one but his widow believed that Filippo could possibly have survived. They were passionately in love, you see, and Adriana always claimed she would know, in her heart, if her husband were no longer alive. She felt most strongly that he was still with her, and that one day he would return.'

She sighed. 'That's why she had this bench placed here, so she could sit and watch the bay for a blue boat with maroon sails. She came every day to keep her vigil, summer and winter, and she refused to listen to any arguments against it. "One day, he will come back to me," she used to say. "And he will find me waiting."'

'How awful,' Marisa said softly. 'Poor woman.'

Mrs Morton smiled again. 'She didn't see herself at all in that way, by all accounts. She was very calm, very steadfast, and doing what she believed in. As well as love, you see, she had faith and hope, so maybe she was one of the lucky ones.'

'What happened in the end?' Marisa asked.

'She caught a chill, which she neglected, and which turned to pneumonia. She was taken to hospital, much against her will, and died a few days later.' She added with faint dryness, 'It's said her last words were "Tell him I waited," which one can believe or not.'

She put on her gloves and rose. 'But this is far too lovely a day, and you're much too young and pretty for any more sad stories about lost love. And I must get on with some work.' She looked again at the sea. 'However, this is a wonderful spot—especially to sit and think—and I hope I haven't depressed you so much that you never come back.'

'No,' Marisa said. 'I'd love to come and sit here— as long as I won't be in the way.'

'On the contrary, I think we can peacefully co-exist.'

'And I have to say that it doesn't actually feel sad at all.'

'Nor to me,' Mrs Morton agreed. 'But I know some of the local people tend to avoid it.'

Marisa said slowly, 'You said, when you saw me, that you thought for a moment Adriana had come back. Is that what people think?'

Behind her spectacles, Mrs Morton's eyes twinkled. 'Not out loud. The parish priest is very against super-stition.' She paused. 'But I was surprised to see you, because so very few visitors come here. In fact, I always think of it as the village's best-kept secret.'

'Yet they told me?' Marisa said, half to herself.

'Well, perhaps you seemed like someone who needed a quiet place to think in the sunshine.' As she moved away Mrs Morton glanced back over her shoulder. 'But that, my dear, is entirely your own business.'

And co-exist, we did, Marisa thought, looking back with a pang of gratitude.

It had been late afternoon when she'd finally returned to Villa Santa Caterina, and she had fully expected to be cross-examined about her absence—by Evangelina if no one else, particularly as she'd failed to return to the villa for lunch. But not a word was said.

And no questions had been asked when she'd announced the following day that she was going for another walk, or any of the days that followed, when she'd climbed the hill to the house, passing her hours quietly on Adriana's bench. She read, and sketched, and tried to make sense of what had happened to her and where it might lead.

Keeping, she realised now, a vigil of her own.

She'd invariably been aware of Mrs Morton's relaxed presence elsewhere in the garden, and sometimes they had chatted, when the older woman took a break from her endeavours, having kindly but firmly refused Marisa's diffident offer of help.

Conversation between them had been restricted to general topics, although Marisa had been aware that sometimes her companion watched her in a faintly puzzled way, as if wondering why she should choose to spend so much time alone.

Once, indeed, she'd asked, 'Do your friends not mind seeing so little of you, my dear?'

'No, not at all.' Marisa looked down at her bare hand. 'We're not—close.'

And then, in the final week of the honeymoon, all her silent questioning was ended when she woke with stomach cramps and realised there would be no baby.

Realised, too, that she would somehow have to go to Renzo and tell him. And then, on some future occasion, steel herself to have sex with him again.

Both of those being prospects that filled her with dread.

She took some painkillers and spent most of the morning in bed, informing Evangelina that she had a headache, probably through too much sun.

'Perhaps you would tell the *signore*,' she added, hoping that Renzo would read between the lines of the message and guess the truth. That as a result she might be spared the embarrassment of a personal interview with him. But Evangelina looked surprised.

'He is not here, *signora*. He has business in Naples and will not return before dinner. Did he not say?'

'I expect so.' Marisa kept her tone light. *Let's keep up the pretence,* she thought, *that this is a normal marriage, where people talk to each other. After all, in a few more days we'll be leaving.* 'I—probably forgot.'

In a way she was relieved at his absence, but knew that her reprieve was only temporary, and that eventually she would have to confront him with the unwelcome truth.

By which time, she told herself unhappily, she might have thought of something to say.

The business in Naples must have taken longer than Renzo had bargained for, because for the first time Marisa was down to dinner ahead of him. And when he did join her he was clearly preoccupied.

She sat quietly, forcing herself to eat and making no attempt to break the silence between them.

But when the coffee arrived and he rose, quietly excusing himself on the grounds that he had phone calls to make, she knew she couldn't delay any longer.

She said, 'Can they wait for a few moments, please? I—I'd like to talk to you.'

'An unexpected honour.' His voice was cool, but he stood, waiting.

She flushed. 'Not really. I—I'm afraid I have—bad news for you. I found out this morning that I'm—not pregnant after all.' She added stiltedly, 'I'm—sorry.'

'Are you?' His tone was expressionless. 'Well, that is understandable.'

She wanted to tell him that wasn't what she meant. That, however it had been conceived, during the weeks of waiting to her own astonishment the baby had somehow become very real to her—and in some strange way precious.

And that this had come home to her most forcefully today, when she'd had to face the fact that his child had never actually existed, and had found herself in the extremity of a different kind of pain.

She said with difficulty, 'You must be very disappointed.'

His faint smile was as bleak as winter. 'I think I am beyond disappointment, Marisa. Perhaps we should discuss this—and other matters—in the morning. Now, you must excuse me.'

When he had gone, Marisa sat staring at the candleflame, sipping her coffee and feeling it turn to bitterness in her throat. Then she pushed the cup away from her, so violently that some of its contents spilled across the white cloth, and went to her bedroom.

She undressed, cleaned her teeth, and put on her nightgown, moving like an automaton. She got into bed and drew the covers around her as if the night was cold. The cramps had subsided long ago, and in their place was a great hollowness.

It's gone, she thought. *My little boy. My little girl. Someone to love, who'd have loved me in return. Who'd have belonged to me.*

Except it was only a figment of my imagination. And I'm left with nothing. No one.

Until the next time, if he can ever bring himself to touch me again.

Suddenly all the pent-up hurt and loneliness of her situation overwhelmed her, and she began to cry, softly at first, and then in hard, choking sobs that threatened to tear her apart.

Leaving her, at last, drained and shivering in the total isolation of that enormous bed.

CHAPTER SEVEN

AND the following morning she had found that her honeymoon had come to an abrupt end.

Her confrontation with Renzo had taken place, to her discomfort, in the *salotto*—a room she'd tried to avoid ever since...since that day, and where she'd managed never to be alone with him again.

She had sat. He had stood, his face bleak, almost haggard. The golden eyes sombre.

He'd spoken quietly, but with finality, while she had stared down at her hands, gripped together in her lap.

As they were now, she noticed, while her memory was recreating once again everything he'd said to her.

He had wasted no time getting to the point. 'I feel strongly, Marisa, that we need to reconsider the whole question of our marriage. I therefore suggest that we leave Villa Santa Caterina either later today or tomorrow, as no useful purpose can be served by our remaining here. Do you agree?'

She hadn't wholly trusted her voice, so it had seemed safer just to nod.

When he had resumed, his voice had been harder.

'I also propose that we spend some time apart from each other, in order to examine our future as husband and wife. Clearly things cannot continue as they are. Decisions will need to be made, and some consensus reached.'

He'd paused. 'You may, of course, take as much time as you need. You need not fear that I shall pressure you in any way. Therefore I am quite willing to stay at my apartment in Rome, and make our home in Tuscany available to you for your sole occupation.'

'No!' She had seen his head go back, and realised how vehement her negation had been. 'I mean— thank you. But under the circumstances that's impossible. Your father will expect to see us together.' She took a deep breath. 'So, I would very much prefer to go back to London. If that can be arranged.'

'London?' he'd repeated. He had looked at her, his eyes narrowing in faint disbelief. 'You mean you wish to rejoin your cousin?'

All hell, Marisa had thought, would freeze over first. But she'd glimpsed a chance of escape, and had known a more moderate answer might achieve a better result.

She'd shaken her head. 'She's moving to Kent very soon, so the question doesn't arise.' She'd paused. 'What I really want, *signore*, is a place of my own. Somewhere just for myself,' she'd added with emphasis. 'With no one else involved.'

There had been a silence, then Renzo had said carefully, 'I see. But—in London? Do you think that is wise?'

'Why not?' Marisa had lifted her chin. 'After all, I'm not a child any more.' *Or your tame virgin, who has to be protected from all predators but you,* her eyes had said, and she'd watched faint colour burn along his cheekbones.

'Besides,' she'd added, her voice challenging. 'If you have an apartment in Rome, why shouldn't I have a flat in London?'

Renzo had spread his hands. He'd said, almost ruefully, 'I can think of a string of reasons, although I doubt you would find any of them acceptable.'

'Nevertheless, that is my choice.' She'd looked down at her hands again. 'And as we'll be living apart anyway, I don't see what difference it can make.'

There had been another pause, then he'd said quietly, 'Very well. Let it be as you wish.'

For a moment she'd felt stunned. She had certainly not expected so easy a victory.

Unless, of course, he simply wanted her out of sight—and out of mind—and as quickly as possible...

For a moment, her feeling of triumph had seemed to ebb, and she'd felt oddly forlorn.

Yet wasn't that exactly what she wanted too? she'd rallied herself. So why should she care?

She had looked at him. Forced a smile. *'Grazie.'*

'Prego.' He had not returned the smile. 'Now, if you

will excuse me, there are arrangements to be made.'
And he'd gone.

After that, Marisa recalled, things had seemed to
happen very fast.

Renzo, it appeared, only had to snap his fingers and
a first-class flight to London became available.
Arrangements were made for a chauffeur and limousine to meet her at the airport, together with a represen-
tative from the Santangelis' UK lawyers. He or she
would be responsible for escorting her to a suite at a
top hotel, which had been reserved for her as a temporary residence, before providing her with a list of
suitable properties and smoothing her path through the
various viewings. Money, of course, being no object.

In fact, she found herself thinking with a pang, as
her plane took off and she waved away the offered
champagne, what wouldn't Renzo pay to be rid of the
girl who'd so signally failed him as a wife?

Because this had to be the beginning of the end of
their marriage, and his lawyers would soon be receiv-
ing other, more personal instructions concerning her.

And she would be free—able for the first time
to make a life for herself as Marisa Brendon.
Answerable, she told herself, to no one. Least of all
to her erstwhile husband, now breathing a sigh of
relief in Rome.

Her only regret was that she hadn't had time to pay
a final visit to Casa Adriana and say goodbye to Mrs
Morton. But perhaps it was better this way.

Those warm, quiet days in the garden had begun to assume a dreamlike quality all their own. Even when she had been entirely alone there, she thought, in some strange way she had never felt lonely.

She did not believe that Adriana's ghost had ever returned, but perhaps love and hope still lingered somehow. And they'd been her comfort.

Once established in London, she had not expected to hear from Renzo again, so his phone calls and letters had come as a distinct shock. A courteous gesture, she'd told herself, that she needed like a hole in the head and could safely ignore.

And now here he was in person, suddenly and without warning. Back in her life, she thought with anger, because in reality he'd never had the slightest intention of letting her go.

Her 'breathing space' was over and there was nothing she could do about it.

Because he clearly had no intention of giving her the divorce she'd been counting on, and she had no resources for a long legal battle.

The first of many bitter pills she would probably have to swallow.

Besides—she owed him, she told herself unhappily. There was no getting away from that. Morally, as well as fiscally, she was obligated to him.

And now, however belatedly, it was indeed payback time.

Was this the so-called consensus he'd offered that day at Villa Santa Caterina? she asked herself bitterly, then paused, knowing that she was banging her head against a wall.

What was the point of going back over all this old ground and reliving former unhappiness?

It was the here and now that mattered.

And she couldn't escape the fact that she'd gone into their marriage with her eyes open, knowing that he did not love her and recognising exactly what was expected of her.

So, in that way, nothing had changed.

This was the life she'd accepted, and somehow she had to live it. And on his terms.

But now she desperately needed to sleep, before tomorrow became today and she was too tired to deal with all the difficulties and demands she didn't even want to contemplate.

And this chair was hardly the right place for that.

With a sigh, she rose and crossed to the bed. As she slipped back under the covers it occurred to her that this might be one of the last nights she would spend alone for some time.

Something else, she told herself grimly, that she did not need to contemplate. Yet.

And she turned over, burying her face in the pillow, seeking for oblivion and discovering gratefully that, in spite of everything, it was waiting for her.

* * *

She awoke as usual, a few moments before her alarm clock sounded, reaching out a drowsy hand to silence it in advance. Then paused, suddenly aware that there was something not quite right about this wakening.

Her heart pounding, Marisa lifted her head and turned slowly and with infinite caution to look at the bed beside her. And paused, stifling an instinctive gasp of shock, when she saw she was no longer alone.

Because Renzo was there, lying on his side, facing away from her and fast asleep, his breathing deep and even, the covers pushed down to reveal every graceful line of his naked back.

Oh, God, Marisa thought, swallowing. *Oh, God, I don't believe this. When did he arrive, and how could I not know about it?*

And why didn't I spend the night in that bloody chair after all?

A fraction of an inch at a time, she began to move towards the edge of the bed, desperate to make her escape before he woke too.

But it was too late, she realised, freezing. Because he was already stirring and stretching, making her vividly conscious of the play of muscle under his smooth tanned skin, before turning towards her.

He propped himself casually on one elbow and studied her, his eyes quizzical. *'Buon giorno.'*

'Good morning be damned.' She found her voice. 'What the hell are you doing here?'

He had the gall to look faintly surprised. 'Getting some rest, *mia cara*. What else?'

'But you said—you promised that you'd sleep on the sofa.'

'Sadly, the sofa had other ideas,' Renzo drawled. 'And I decided that I valued my spine too much to argue any longer.'

'Well, you had no right,' she said hoarsely. 'No right at all to—to march in here like this and—and—help yourself!'

His brows lifted. 'I did not march, *mia bella*. I moved very quietly so I would not disturb you. And I did not, as you continued to sleep soundly.'

He paused. 'Besides, as a good wife, surely you do not begrudge me a little comfort, *carissima*?' He added softly, 'After all, despite considerable temptation, I made no attempt to take anything more.'

'I am not a good wife.' Totally unnerved by the tone of his voice, and the look in his eyes, she uttered the stupid, *stupid* words before she could stop herself, and saw his smile widen hatefully into a grin of sheer delight.

'Not yet, perhaps,' he agreed, unforgivably. 'But I live in hope that when you discover how good a husband I intend to be your attitude may change.'

Marisa realised his eyes were now lingering disturbingly on her shoulders, bare under the narrow straps of her nightdress, and then moving down to the slight curve of her breasts revealed by its demure cotton bodice.

Her throat tightened. *I have to get him out of here,* she thought. *Not just out of this bed, but this room too. Before I make an even bigger fool of myself.*

'But as we are here together,' he went on musingly. 'It occurs to me that maybe I should teach you what a man most desires when he wakes in the morning with his wife beside him.'

He reached out, brushing the strap down from her shoulder, letting his fingertips caress the faint mark it had left on her skin. It was the lightest of touches, but she felt it blaze like wildfire through her blood, sending her every sense quivering.

Suddenly she found herself remembering their wedding night, and that devastating, electrifying moment when she'd experienced the first stroke of his hand on her naked breast.

Dry-mouthed, she said, 'No, Renzo—please.' And despised herself for the note of entreaty in her voice.

'But I must, *mia bella*,' he murmured. 'Don't you think I have waited quite long enough to instruct you in my needs? What I like—and how I like it?'

She tried to think of something to say and failed completely. She was aware that he'd moved close, and knew she should draw back—distance herself before it was too late.

'Because it is quite simple,' the softly compelling voice went on. 'I require it to be very hot, very black, and very strong—without sugar. Even you can manage that, I think.'

Marisa shot bolt upright, glaring at him. 'Coffee,' she said, her voice almost choking on the word. 'You're saying you want me to—make you—coffee?' She drew a stormy breath. 'Well, in your dreams, *signore*. I don't know what your last slave died of, but you know where the kitchen is, so make your own damned drink.'

Renzo lay back against the pillows, watching her from under lowered lids. 'Not the response I had hoped for, *carissima*.' His drawl held amusement. He glanced past her at the clock. 'However, I see it is still early, so maybe I will forgo the coffee and persuade you to join me in a little gentle exercise instead. Would you prefer that?' Another pause. 'Or has the kitchen suddenly become more attractive to you after all?'

She said thickly, 'Bastard,' and scrambled out of bed with more haste than dignity, grabbing at her robe. She was followed to the door by the sound of his laughter.

Once in the kitchen, she closed the door and leaned against it while she steadied her breathing.

Renzo had been winding her up, she thought incredulously, subjecting her to some light-hearted sexual teasing, and it was a side of him she hadn't seen before.

Or not since the night of her birthday dinner, she amended, swallowing, when his eyes and the touch of his mouth on her hand had asked questions she'd been too scared to answer and once again she'd run away.

A girl does not have to be in love with a man to enjoy what he does to her in bed. His own words, and he clearly believed them.

But it isn't true, she thought, her throat tightening. *Not for me. Simply wanting someone isn't enough, and never could be. I'd have to be in love to in order to give myself, and even then there'd have to be trust—and respect as well.*

Things that Renzo had probably never heard of as he swanned his way through life from bed to bed.

Besides, he didn't really want her. She was simply a means to an end. But what happened on their honeymoon obviously still rankled with him. For once his seduction routine hadn't worked, and with his wife of all people.

His pride had been damaged, and he couldn't allow that, so now he didn't only want a son from her, but an addition to his list of conquests. To have her panting to fall into his arms each time he walked through the door.

Well, I don't need this, she thought fiercely. *I've no interest in his technique as a lover, and I won't let myself be beguiled into wanting him. It's not going to happen.*

I'm going to be the one that got away. The one that proves to him, as well as myself, that there is life after Lorenzo Santangeli.

She filled the kettle and set it to boil, noting with rebellious satisfaction that there was no fresh coffee. So he'd have to drink instant and like it.

She spooned granules into a beaker, then glanced

around her, wondering what would happen to her little domain when she returned to Italy. It was hardly likely she'd be able to retain it as a bolthole when her role as Santangeli wife and future mother became too much to bear.

Although she supposed she could always ask. Because she'd need somewhere eventually, after she'd given Renzo his heir and became surplus to requirements.

In fact, she could impose a few conditions of her own on her return to him, she thought. Let him know that her acquiescence to his wishes now, and later, was still open to negotiation.

Not just a place to live, she told herself, but a purpose in life, too. For afterwards…

In painful retrospect, she'd worked out that any plans she might have for her eventual child—the bond she'd once envisaged—would be little more than fantasy.

She'd seen the stately nurseries at the Santangeli family home, and knew that once she'd given birth her work would be over. There'd be no breastfeeding or nappy-changing for Signora Santangeli. The baby would be handed over to a hierarchy of doting staff who would answer its cries, be the recipients of its first smile, supervise the tooth-cutting and the initial wobbly steps, with herself little more than a bystander.

So she'd be left to her own devices, she thought bleakly, in Julia's classic phrase. And would need something to fill her time and assuage the ache in her heart.

And quite suddenly she knew what it could be, what she would ask in return for her wifely compliance.

Simple, she thought. Neat and beautiful. Now all she required was Renzo's agreement, which could be trickier.

The coffee made, she carried the brimming beaker back to the bedroom. But it was empty, the covers on the bed thrown back.

He was in the adjoining bathroom, standing at the basin, shaving, a towel knotted round his hips and his dark hair still damp from the shower.

'You haven't wasted any time.' Self-consciously she stepped forward, and put the beaker within his reach.

'I wish I could say the same of you, *mia cara*.' His tone was dry. 'I thought you had gone to pick the beans.' He tasted the brew and winced slightly. 'But clearly not.'

'I'm sorry if it doesn't meet your exacting standards.'

Damn, she thought. In view of what she was about to ask, a more conciliatory note might be an improvement.

He rinsed his razor and laid it aside. 'Well, it is hot,' he said. 'And I am grateful for that, at least. *Grazie, carissima.*'

And before she could read his intention, or take evading action, his arm snaked out, drawing her swiftly against him, and he was kissing her startled mouth, his lips warm and delicately sensuous as they moved on hers.

The scent of his skin, the fragrance of the soap he'd

used, were suddenly all around her, and she felt as if she was breathing him, absorbing him through every pore, as he held her in the strong curve of his arm.

And she waited, her heart hammering, for his kiss to deepen. To demand…

Then, with equal suddenness, she was free again. She took an instinctive step backwards on legs that were not entirely steady, the colour storming into her face as she met his ironic gaze.

'So,' he said. 'We make progress, *mia bella*. We have not only shared a bed, but I have kissed you at last.' He collected his razor and toothbrush, and put them in his wash-bag, then walked to the door, where he paused.

He said gently, 'You were worth waiting for, Maria Lisa,' and went out, leaving her staring after him.

If there had to be only one door in the flat with a bolt on it, she was glad it was the bathroom.

Not that she would be interrupted. Instinct told her that Renzo would not try to make immediate capital out of what had just happened, but would leave her to wait—and wonder.

Which, of course, she would, she thought, gritting her teeth.

She'd always known it would be dangerous to allow him too close, and she could see now that her wariness had been fully justified.

He was—lethal, she thought helplessly.

Yet even she could see it was ridiculous to be so profoundly disturbed by something that had lasted only a few seconds at most.

Her only comfort was that she had not kissed him back, but had stayed true to her convictions by remaining passive in his embrace.

But he was the one who stopped, a small, niggling voice in her head reminded her. *So don't congratulate yourself too soon.*

Showered and dressed in her working clothes, with her hair drawn back from her face and secured at the nape of her neck with a silver clip, she emerged from the bathroom, mentally steeling herself for the next encounter.

Cool unresponsiveness would seem to be the answer, she thought, but a lot might depend on how the question was asked.

A reflection that sent an odd shiver tingling through her body.

But it seemed there was to be no immediate confrontation because, to her surprise, Renzo wasn't there. The only sign of his presence was the neatly folded blanket, topped by the pillow, on the sofa.

She stood looking round her in bewilderment, wondering if by some miracle he'd suddenly decided to cut his losses and leave for Italy alone.

But it wasn't a day for miracles, because his travel bag was still there, standing in the hall.

On the other hand, she thought, she could always fling a few things together herself, and vanish before he returned. There had to be places where the Santangeli influence didn't reach—although she couldn't call any of them to mind.

And with that she heard the sound of a key in the flat door and Renzo came in, dangling a bulging plastic carrier bag from one lean hand.

Marisa stared at it, then him. 'You've been shopping?'

'Evidently. I found the contents of your refrigerator singularly uninspiring, *mia bella.*'

'But there's nowhere open,' she protested. 'It's too early.'

'Shops are always glad of customers. This one was no exception.' He held up the bag, emblazoned with the name of a local delicatessen. 'I saw a light on and knocked. They were perfectly willing to serve me.'

'Oh, naturally,' Marisa said grittily. 'How could anyone refuse the great Lorenzo Santangeli?'

'That,' he said gently, 'is a question that you can answer better than anyone, *carissima.*' He paused. 'Now, shall we have breakfast?'

She wanted to refuse haughtily, furious at having been caught leading with her chin yet again, but she could smell the enticing aroma of warm bread and realised that she was starving.

He'd bought ham, cheese, sausage and fresh rolls, she found, plus a pack of rich aromatic coffee.

They ate at the small breakfast bar in the kitchen, and in spite of everything Marisa discovered it was one of the few meals she'd enjoyed in his company.

Renzo poured himself some more coffee and glanced at his watch. 'It is almost time we were leaving. There are a number of things to be attended to before we leave for the airport, and you have yet to pack.'

'That won't take very long,' she said. 'I haven't many clothes.'

'No?' he asked dryly. 'You forget, *mia cara*, that I remember how many cases you brought with you to England.'

She bit her lip. 'Actually,' she said, trying to sound casual, 'I don't have those things any more.'

'You had better explain.'

'I gave all my trousseau away,' she admitted uncomfortably. 'To various charity shops. And the luggage too.'

'In the name of God, why?' He looked at her as if she had grown a second head.

'Because I didn't think I'd need clothes like that any more,' she said defiantly. 'So I'll just have one bag.'

'Very well.' His voice held a touch of grimness. 'Then let us start by going to this place where you have been working. Handing in your notice will take the least time.'

It wasn't the ideal moment after her last revelation, Marisa thought, but it was still now or never.

She cleared her throat. 'Actually, the visit may take rather longer than that. You see, there's something I need to—discuss with you first.'

'About the gallery?' Renzo put the knife he'd been

using back on his plate with almost studied care. 'Or its owner?'

'Well—both,' she said, slightly taken aback.

'I am listening,' he said harshly. 'But are you sure you want me to hear?'

'Yes, of course. Because it's important.' She took a deep breath. 'I want—I mean I would really like you to buy me—a half-share in the Estrello.'

There was a silence, then he said, almost grimly. 'You dare ask me that? You really believe I would be willing to give money to your lover?'

Marisa gasped. 'Lover?' she echoed in disbelief. 'You think that Corin—and I...? Oh, God, that's so absurd.' She faced him, eyes sparking with anger. 'He's a decent man having a bad time, that's all.'

She paused, then added very deliberately. 'I don't have a lover, *signore*, and I never have done. As no one should know better than yourself.'

Renzo looked away, and for the second time in her life she saw him flush. 'Then what is your interest in this place?'

'Corin's wife is divorcing him, and she wants a financial stake in the gallery. She's not interested in artists or pictures, just in the Estrello's potential as a redevelopment site. She's even planning to work there after they're divorced, so she can pressure him into selling up altogether.'

'And he will do this?' Renzo asked. 'Why does he not fight back?'

'Because he still loves her,' Marisa said fiercely. 'I don't suppose you can imagine what it would be like for him, being forced to see her each day under those circumstances.'

'Perhaps I am not as unimaginative as you believe,' Renzo said, after another pause. 'However, I still do not understand why you should wish to involve yourself—or me.'

'For one thing it's successful,' she said. 'So it would be a good investment.' She hesitated. 'For another, being part-owner will provide me with an interest—even a future career, which I'm going to need some day.'

His brows lifted sardonically. 'It does not occur to you that some wives seem to find a satisfactory career in their marriages—their families?'

'But not,' she said, 'when they know the position is on a strictly temporary basis.' She paused. 'Shall I go on?'

'Please do. I assure you I am fascinated.'

'Thirdly,' she said, 'Corin really needs the money. He would be so thankful for help.' She looked away, biting her lip. 'And I would be grateful too, of course.'

'Ah,' he said softly. 'And what form would this gratitude take? Or is it indelicate to ask?'

It was her turn to flush. 'I think it's a little late for delicacy.'

'Then tell me.'

She stared down fixedly at her empty plate. 'I'll go

back to Italy with you—as your wife. And give you—whatever you want.'

'However reluctantly,' he said softly. 'A new feast day should be proclaimed. The martyrdom of Santa Marisa.'

'That's unfair.'

'Is it?' His mouth twisted. 'As to that, we shall both have to wait and see.' He paused. 'But this is the price of your—willing return to me?'

She lifted her chin. Met his gaze unflinchingly. 'Yes.'

'And your uncomplaining presence in my bed when I require it?'

'Yes.' She forced herself to say it.

'*Incredibile*,' he said mockingly. 'Then naturally I accept. If I can agree to terms with this Corin, who needs another man's wife to fight his battles for him.'

She was about to protest that that was unfair too. That it was not just for Corin, but herself, and her life after marriage, but she realised it would be wiser to keep quiet. So she contented herself with a stilted, 'Thank you.'

Renzo got to his feet, and she rose too. As she went past him to the door he took her arm, swinging her round to face him.

He said unsmilingly, 'You set a high price on your favours, *mia bella*. So this is a bargain you will keep. *Capisci?*'

She nodded silently, and he released her with a swift, harsh sigh.

But as she followed him out of the room she realised that she was trembling inside, and she thought, *What have I done? Oh, dear God, what have I done?*

CHAPTER EIGHT

'DEAR child.' Guillermo Santangeli kissed Marisa on both cheeks, then stood back to regard her fondly. 'You look beautiful, although a little thin. I hope you are not on some silly diet.'

'No, I'm fine,' she returned awkwardly, embarrassed by the open affection in his greeting. It was as if the last painful months had never happened, she thought, bewildered, and she was simply returning home, a radiant wife, from her honeymoon. 'But Renzo told me what happened to you, and I was—worried.'

Her father-in-law shrugged expansively. 'A small inconvenience, no more. But it made me feel my age, and that was not good.' His arm round her shoulders, he took her into the *salotto*. Renzo followed, his face expressionless. 'Now that you are here I shall recover completely, *figlia mia.*

'You remember Signora Alesconi, I hope?' he added, as a tall, beautiful woman rose from one of the deep armchairs.

'That is hardly likely, Guillermo.' The older woman's handshake was as warm as her smile. 'I attended your wedding, Signora Santangeli, but I do not expect you to recall one person among so many. So let us count this as our true meeting.' She turned, her expression becoming more formal. 'It is also a pleasure to see you again, Signor Lorenzo,' she added, as he bowed over her hand.

'And I, *signora*, am glad to have this opportunity to thank you for acting so quickly when my father became ill,' Renzo returned. 'Please believe that I shall always be grateful.' He smiled at her. 'And that it is good to see you here.'

'We are indeed a family party,' his father remarked, studying an apparent fleck on his fingernail. 'Nonna Teresa arrived this afternoon. She is resting in her room at present, but will join us for dinner.'

There was a pause, then Renzo said expressionlessly, 'Now, that is a joy I did not anticipate.'

'Nor I,' said Guillermo, and father and son exchanged level looks.

Marisa felt her heart plummet. Of all the Santangeli connections, Renzo's grandmother had always been the least friendly, dismissing the proposed marriage as 'insupportable sentiment' and 'dangerous nonsense'.

And although Marisa had privately agreed with her views, it had still not been pleasant hearing her total unsuitability voiced aloud—and with such venom.

And now the *signora* was here—apparently uninvited—on what promised to be the most difficult night of her entire life.

Following, as it did, one of the most difficult days.

But for the emotional turmoil that had had her in its grip, the events at the Estrello Gallery that morning might almost have been amusing, she thought, as she took a seat and accepted the cup of coffee that Signora Alesconi poured for her.

Corin's face had been a study when she'd broken the news that she was leaving, and why. And when finally, with trepidation, she had introduced an un-smiling Renzo as her husband, explaining that the problem of the gallery's future might have a solution, the whole encounter had almost tipped over into farce.

Almost, she thought, swallowing, but not quite.

She'd been thankful to leave the pair of them to talk business in Corin's cubbyhole of an office while she cleared her few personal items from her desk.

But her feelings had been mixed when Corin had emerged, clearly pole-axed, to tell her the deal was done and it was now down to the lawyers.

Because it had not simply been a matter of le-galities, and she had known that. And so had the man who'd stood behind Corin, watching her, his dark face uncompromising. The husband who would seek rec-ompense by claiming his right to her body that night.

'So—partner.' Corin had given her a wavering smile. 'I guess it's hail and farewell—for a while, anyway.' He shook his head. 'God, I can hardly believe it. I—I don't know how to thank you. Both of you,' he added, sending a faintly apprehensive glance back at Renzo.

Then he brightened. 'Perhaps you'll let me give you something to mark the occasion—a combined wedding present and goodbye gift, eh?'

And before Marisa could stop him he went over to the wall and lifted down the Amalfi picture.

'I've often seen you looking at this,' he confided cheerfully. 'I realise now that it may have been reviving some happy memories.'

'A most generous thought,' Renzo interposed smoothly as Marisa's lips parted in instinctive protest. 'My wife and I will treasure it.'

'Treasure it?' Marisa queried almost hoarsely a little later, as the picture, well cushioned by bubble-wrap and brown paper, shared the opulent rear of the limousine that was taking them to Renzo's next appointment at the London branch of the Santangeli Bank. 'I'd like to put my fist through it.' She shook her head. 'God, how could you say such a thing? Tell such a downright lie?'

His brows lifted. 'Did you wish me to tell him the unhappy truth?' he enquired coolly. 'Besides, it is a beautiful scene, very well painted. I have no objection to owning it. However, if you prefer, I will hang it where you are unlikely to see it.' He paused, adding sardonically, 'In my bedroom, perhaps.'

She sat back, bright spots of colour blazing in her cheeks, unable to think of a riposte that wouldn't lead to worse embarrassment.

After a pause, Renzo went on, 'So, Marisa, as you wished, you now have a half-share in a London gallery.'

She did not look at him. 'And you have me.'

'Do I?' His tone was reflective. 'I think that has yet to be proved, *mia bella*.'

He added, more briskly, 'If there is anything you wish to take from the flat apart from your clothes then you should make a list. I will have them sent on to us. After our departure the place will be cleared for re-letting.'

'Oh.' She bit her lip. 'I hoped I—we—might keep it. Maybe as a *pied à terre* for visits to London.' She paused. 'It could be useful, don't you think?'

'I am sure, in time, you will prefer less cramped surroundings.'

And that, she realised resentfully, was that. Renzo had made his final concession. From now on it would be her turn. And she shivered.

Later, he watched while she packed, and she saw his mouth tighten when he observed the few basic items that her wardrobe contained, but he made no further comment.

Possibly, she thought, because for once he was lost for words. Or calculating how much it would cost him to re-equip her for her unwanted role.

No! Her self-reproach was instant and whole-hearted. That was totally unfair. If money was all it took to make her happy, then by now she'd be ecstatic, because in material ways she'd lacked for nothing from the very beginning.

Kept in the lap of luxury, she told herself derisively.

And knew she would not be the first to discover how lonely and unrewarding that could be.

As she sat beside him on the way to the airport, trying to present at least an appearance of calm, he was the first to break the silence between them.

'Our flight is booked to Pisa, but I am wondering whether Rome would not be a better option.' He paused, glancing at her. 'A transfer is easily arranged. We could spend a few days at my apartment and then travel to Tuscany at the weekend.'

A few days, she thought, her throat tightening. And a few nights—alone with him.

A situation which bore all the hallmarks of a second honeymoon, but the same propensity for disaster as the first. In an apartment that she'd never seen, and which might not have the separate bedrooms which offered at least a semblance of privacy at the Villa Proserpina.

And then, with dizzying abruptness, she found herself remembering those few brief moments earlier that day, when his arms had held her and his lips had touched hers for the first time.

When she'd experienced the hard, lean warmth of his body against hers and realised, in a blazing instant of self-knowledge, that she didn't want him to let her go…

And she wondered if he had known it too.

Shock jolted her like a charge of electricity. *No*, she protested in silent horror. *Oh, please, no. That didn't happen. It couldn't happen. I'm just uptight, that's all. And the kiss took me by surprise.*

She said, too quickly, 'But your father's expecting us. He'll be disappointed if we break our journey like that.'

'You are all consideration, *mia bella*. *Tuttavia*, I think, given the circumstances, he would completely understand.' He added with faint amusement, *'In effetti*, he could even be pleased.'

Her heart missed a beat. 'But I would still worry,' she said. 'After all, he's been ill. And I want to see him. So maybe we should stick to the original arrangement.'

There was a brief silence before he said quietly, 'Then let it be as you wish.'

As I wish? she thought, with a mixture of bewilderment and desperation, as new tensions—new forebodings—began to twist themselves into a knot in her mind. *Dear God, suddenly I don't know what I wish— not any more. And that really scares me.*

Because nothing had changed. That kiss had simply been to prove a point. Unfinished business, that was all. Because he'd made no attempt to put a hand on her since. Even sitting side by side in the back of the car like this, he was making sure there was a distinct space between them.

But, she thought, swallowing, all that would change tonight. There was no escaping that harsh reality. And she'd had that softly arousing brush of his mouth on hers to warn her what she might expect.

She was trembling inside again, bleak with an apprehension she couldn't dismiss, and in spite of the comfort of the flight, and the assiduous attentions of the cabin staff, she found herself developing a headache.

However, as she reminded herself tautly, it would hardly be politic, in the current situation, to mention the fact—even if he believed her. Better, indeed, to suffer in silence than to be treated with icy mockery. Or anger again.

No, she thought, please—not anger.

And she closed her eyes, wincing.

They were met at Galileo Galilei airport by her father-in-law's own sumptuous limousine and its chauffeur, who, with due deference, handed Renzo a briefcase as he took his seat.

'You will excuse me, *mia cara*?' He spoke, she thought, as if the flight had been an endless exchange of sweet nothings, instead of several more edgy hours almost totally lacking in conversation. 'There are some urgent messages I must read.'

Huddled in her corner, Marisa observed some of the most exquisite scenery in Europe with eyes that saw nothing. Maybe one of the messages would summon him immediately to the other side of the globe, she thought, without particular hope.

But he went through the sheaf of papers swiftly, scribbling notes in the margins as he went, then returned them to the briefcase just as the car turned in between the tall stone pillars and took the long avenue lined with cypresses leading to the gracious mass of pinkish-grey stone that formed the Villa Proserpina.

All too soon they'd arrived at what would be her home for the foreseeable future, and as if things weren't quite bad enough Teresa Barzati had to be waiting for them, like a thin, autocratic spider that had invaded and occupied a neighbouring web.

But we could have been elsewhere, of course, Marisa reminded herself bitterly, sitting on the edge of her chair, tension in every line of her body. *Renzo offered me an alternative, and in retrospect Rome seems marginally the better choice, no matter what I thought at the time. Because no change of location is going to make the obligation of going into his arms— his bed—any easier.*

But it's too late now. Everything's much too late.

Wearily, she pushed her hair back from her face, aware that her head was throbbing badly now, and she was almost grateful when her untouched cup was taken from her hand and Renzo said quietly, 'You have had a long day, Marisa. Perhaps you might like to follow Nonna Teresa's example and relax for a while in your room?'

Yes, she thought longingly. *Oh, yes!* Some time and space to herself, however brief.

Renzo stepped to the long bell-pull beside the fire-place, and gave succinct instructions in his own language to the uniformed maid who answered its summons.

As a result, only a few minutes later Marisa found herself lying under the silk canopy of the large four-poster bed that dominated her bedroom, divested of her outer clothing and covered by a thin embroidered quilt.

In addition, a cloth soaked in some soothing herbal essence had been placed on her forehead, and she'd been offered two anonymous white tablets and a glass of water to swallow them with.

Even while she was telling herself that relaxation under the circumstances was totally impossible, she went out like a light.

He had never, Renzo thought, felt so nervous. Not even on his wedding day.

He dried his face and applied a little aftershave, reflecting as he did so that his hand had shaken so much while he was carefully removing even the tiniest vestige of stubble from his chin that it was a miracle he'd not cut himself to ribbons.

Like some adolescent, he thought in self-derision, with his first love. Except he was no longer a boy, but a man and a husband, wanting everything to be perfect on this, his real wedding night, with the girl he planned to make his own at last. Somehow…

Yet he was afraid at the same time that it might already be too late for the errors of the past to be forgotten. Or forgiven.

Especially that first disastrous time, which it still shamed him to remember.

Are you saying you want me to make love to you?
He recalled the faint flicker of hope in his question.

Say—yes, he'd prayed silently. *Ah,* Dio, *say yes,* carissima mia, *and let me take us both to heaven.*

Instead, stunned by anger and disappointment, and wounded by her declared indifference, he'd simply taken her without any of the gentleness and respect he'd promised himself he would bring to her initiation, forcing himself to remain grimly oblivious to anything but his own physical necessity.

To appease by that brief and selfish act the aching desire that had tormented him since that moment at her cousin's house when he'd first seen her as a woman. And which had only increased throughout the weeks of self-imposed denial that had followed their engagement.

With hindsight, he knew that in spite of what he'd said afterwards he should have swallowed his pride and gone to her that night, and for both their sakes put matters right between them. That he should have told her that since her acceptance of his proposal there'd been no other girl in his life, that Lucia Gallo was history, and then convinced her that he did indeed want her by devoting himself exclusively to her pleasure until she slept, fulfilled and sated, in his arms.

One small sign—one—over dinner that night that she too had regrets was all it would have taken. But there'd been nothing except that quiet, nervous politeness that had chilled him to the soul.

Leaving him to wonder in anguish whether that afternoon's quick, soulless episode was all she would ever want from him—as much intimacy as she would ever permit. Whether she neither expected nor required any joy or warmth from the uniting of their flesh. Whether her real hope was that pregnancy would release her from any further demands by him.

Forcing him to realise too that she had no more wish to spend her days with him than she did her nights. That she seemed to prefer total solitude to even a moment of his company. Which was perhaps the most hurtful thing of all.

And that was why, when she'd told him in that small, stony voice that after all there would be no baby, it had seemed like a reprieve. As if he'd been given another chance to redeem himself and their marriage, he'd thought, hiding his instinctive thankfulness.

A God-given opportunity to try again.

Evangelina had told him, brow furrowed, that 'the little one' had spent an uncomfortable day, which had given him the excuse he needed to go to her at last. To share her bed, he'd told himself dryly, without even a suspicion of an ulterior motive, and prove to her that he could be capable of real tenderness.

And in doing so accustom her by degrees to his continued presence beside her at night. So that he could tell her gently, at some point, that he wanted their baby made in mutual happiness and delight. Perhaps more.

He'd shaved again that night too, he recalled ironically, before walking resolutely down the length of the dressing room corridor to her door, where he'd paused to knock.

The first time that he'd ever hesitated to enter a woman's bedroom.

And then, as he'd raised his hand, he'd heard her weeping—listened, frozen in shock, to the harsh, agonised sobs reaching him all too clearly through the thick wooden panels—and every thought, wish, desire that had accompanied him from his room to hers had vanished. Leaving in its place a sick, empty void.

Because she couldn't have been crying over a child that had never existed—a child she hadn't even wanted.

No, it was the realisation that eventually she would have to submit to him again—allow her body to be used a second time—that must have released such a terrible storm of grief. Grief, he'd recognised painfully, and revulsion. It could be nothing else.

His worst fears had been horribly justified.

Yet who was to say that anything had changed now—tonight? Renzo asked himself broodingly as he dropped the towel he'd been wearing and put on his robe. What if the morning's bravado suddenly deserted her, and when the time came for her to redeem her promise he found her in tears again?

What would he do then?

Last time he'd returned silently to his room and spent a wretched night sleepless with his regrets, knowing, as dawn approached, that he had to let her go for a while. That he simply did not trust himself to live any longer as they had been doing.

Because there would come a night, he'd told himself with brutal candour, when his need for her might overwhelm him. And he could not risk that.

Of course any separation would be purely temporary. He would make that clear. Then gradually he would resume contact between them, and begin courting her as he should have done from the first.

A laudable ambition, Renzo thought wryly, as he combed his damp hair, but doomed from the moment she'd announced her defiant determination to leave Italy.

He'd accepted that his fight to win her would be conducted from a distance, at least at the start, but he'd never for a moment anticipated crashing headlong into the implacable wall of silence she'd proceeded to build between them from London.

Leaving him struggling a second time against that lethal combination of damaged pride and sheer bad temper that had been his downfall previously.

And proving, he told himself bitterly, that he'd learned precisely nothing in the intervening period.

Because he should, of course, have followed her, preferably on the next flight, and courted her properly. Sweeping away her resentment and resistance until he found her again.

Found Maria Lisa—the girl who'd once looked at him as if he was the sun that warmed her own particular universe.

Every instinct he possessed told him that she had to be there, somewhere, if only he could reach her.

So what had stopped him? The fear, perhaps, that she might still elude him and he could fail?

He did not, after all, take rejection well. So when all his overtures had been ignored he'd looked deliberately for the most practical form of consolation he could find.

And now he was back at the beginning, trying to construct a whole new marriage from the ruins of the old.

The only certainty being that she would not make it easy for him.

She hadn't even trusted him enough to tell him that she'd been in pain on the journey, but he'd seen the strain in her eyes, the way her hand had gone fleetingly to her forehead when she'd thought he wasn't looking, and had taken appropriate action once they'd reached the villa.

But that was the simple part, he thought wryly. Now, somehow, he had to win her.

And for the first time in his life he had no idea how to begin.

Marisa awoke slowly and lay for a moment, feeling totally disorientated. Then, as her head cleared, she remembered where she was. And more importantly, why.

Swallowing, she sat up, pushing the hair back from her face as she stared around her, feeling once more as if she'd been caught in some time warp.

She was again the nervous bride-to-be of the previous year, being shown her future domain by the man who would share these rooms with her. And too embarrassed at the prospect to allow herself more than a fleeting overall glance.

But some details had remained locked in her memory. This huge bed, for instance, with its tapestried canopy and curtains, where eventually she'd be obliged to submit to whatever Renzo asked of her. And those two doors—one leading into the palatial white-and-silver bathroom which they would share, and the other the communicating door into the adjoining room, his room. At present, mercifully closed.

She became aware of other things too. That the shutters over the long windows leading out to the *loggia* were fastened, and their concealing drapes drawn over them. That the pair of deeply shaded lamps that flanked the bed had been lit by someone, too. And all this while she'd slept.

But how long had she been there? She reached for her watch, which had been placed on the night table, but was instantly distracted by the unwelcome sight of the communicating door swinging open and Renzo walking into the room.

Stifling a gasp of dismay, she slid hastily back under the shelter of the coverlet and saw him halt, his brows lifting cynically at the manoeuvre.

Beautifully cut charcoal pants clung to his lean hips and accentuated the length of his legs, and his white shirt hung negligently open, revealing far too much of his muscular brown chest.

In spite of herself Marisa felt her mouth dry, and her heart beginning to thud. She said with faint breathlessness, 'Good—good evening. Did you want something?'

'Certainly not what you seem to expect,' he returned crisply. He looked her over, the golden eyes assimilating the slender shape of her under the concealing coverlet. 'Unless, of course, you insist?'

'I don't!' The denial seemed choked out of her.

He smiled faintly. 'I believe you. But for the present I wish only to speak to you.' He walked over to the bed and stood at its foot, his golden gaze examining her. 'Are you feeling better?'

'Yes—thank you.' Her recent headache seemed to have vanished completely, she realised with surprise. But no doubt there would be many more to take its place. And this interview could be the first.

'I am delighted to hear it.' His tone was silky. 'And I hope you will please my father too, by joining him for dinner.' He paused. 'He wished to make it a black tie celebration in your honour, but has now consented to a less formal affair. I trust that is agreeable to you?'

'Yes,' Marisa said in a hollow voice, reflecting on the deficiencies of her wardrobe. 'Of course.'

He nodded. 'Also the meal will be earlier than usual, as it is considered unwise for Papa to stay up too late. Can you be ready in an hour?'

She fastened her watch back on her wrist. 'I could

probably be ready in five minutes. After all, I'm hardly going to be spoiled for choice over what to wear.'

'One of the reasons I suggested a stopover in Rome,' he said softly. 'So that you could go shopping.' He paused. 'Although not the only reason, of course.'

'No.' She made a slight adjustment to the watch's bracelet, not looking at him. 'I—appreciate that.'

'And we would also have been spared the reception committee,' he went on. 'For which I apologise.'

She did glance up then. In the days leading up to the wedding, in spite of her own inner turmoil, she'd been aware there were other tensions in the household.

She bit her lip. 'Do you no longer mind so much about Signora Alesconi?' she asked in a low voice.

'Ottavia?' There was genuine surprise in his voice. 'No, how could I? What right have I of all people to begrudge my father another chance to be happy?' He paused, then added dryly, 'I did not mean her.'

Marisa took a breath. 'Oh—your grandmother.' She hesitated. 'Considering how little she likes me, I'm surprised she chose to be here.'

Renzo shrugged. 'No doubt she has her reasons. I regret her presence, but you must not allow it to disturb you.'

Your grandmother, signore, she told him silently, *is the least of my worries.*

Aloud, she said tautly, 'She clearly thought I wasn't worthy to be your wife. I expect she thinks so still. And that she's quite right.'

'Not a view I have ever shared.' He hesitated. 'Which is one of the things I came to say to you. We did not begin our marriage well, Maria Lisa, but all that could so easily change—with a little…goodwill, perhaps.'

She stared unseeingly at the embroidery on the coverlet. 'How can it? We're still the same people, after all. Both pushed into this situation by our families,' she added bitterly.

'No one pushed me,' Renzo said quietly. 'It is true that the mothers who loved us both believed that we could be happy together, but that would have counted for nothing if I had wished to choose elsewhere. But—I did not.'

He paused again. '*Tuttavia*, I am aware that for you the choice was not so easy,' he added ruefully. 'That there was—pressure. But if you truly found the idea of our marriage so repulsive then you should have said so—and to me.'

Marisa's lips parted in a gasp of sheer indignation. 'In my dreams,' she said stormily. She propped herself on an elbow, uncaring that the coverlet had slipped down below her lace-cupped breasts. 'And you know it, *signore*. How could I *choose* when I'd been bought and paid for, like any other commodity? And when my cousin's husband's future wellbeing depended on me doing exactly as I was told?'

She drew a breath. 'That was the clincher. Because Harry's sweet and decent in a way you couldn't appreciate, and it was impossible for me to let him down.

So I had to consent to being… handed over—untouched—to the great Lorenzo Santangeli. Someone who'd never given me a second glance until he was reminded of his dynastic obligations and suddenly required a willing virgin.' She added furiously, 'Not many of those to draw on in your social circle, I dare say. So my life had to be wrecked to provide one for you.' She shook her head. 'What a pity I wasn't the slut you once called me.

'At least I'd have been spared…all this.'

There was a silence, then Renzo said slowly, 'That was quite a speech, *mia bella*. How strange that you only speak from the heart when saying things you know I will not wish to hear. But at least now I understand that your resentment of me goes back much further than this past year alone.'

He stood up and walked slowly round the bed to her side.

'You were only fifteen, were you not, when you decided to test my self-control that day in the pool?' He spoke softly. 'And while I do not aspire to your Harry's level of sanctity, I am occasionally capable of a spark of decency—such as not taking advantage of the heedless innocence of a girl hardly out of childhood. If I was harsh with you, it was because I wished to ensure that you would not be lured into making a similar offer to any other man.'

His voice slowed to a husky drawl. 'But do not ever think, Maria Lisa, that I was not tempted. And if I had succumbed to your enticement I would not have merely looked, believe me. Not with a second or even a third glance.'

He sat down on the edge of the bed, and as she tried to move away from him, leaned across to place a hand squarely on the other side of her, trapping her where she lay.

'So what would you have done, *carissima?*' he queried softly, looking into her dilating eyes. 'If you had suddenly found yourself naked with me in the water? And if I had taken you in my arms…?'

'As it didn't happen,' Marisa said curtly, aware that she was trembling, 'this is a totally pointless discussion. And now please let me up.'

'In my own good time,' he said, and had the gall to smile at her. 'Because it is quite clear to me, *mia bella*, that my dismissal of you that day still rankles with you. Therefore it is time I made reparation.'

He bent towards her, his purpose evident, and Marisa reacted, gasping, her hands braced, to her dismay, against the warmth of his bare chest.

'Renzo—please—you can't.'

'Why not?' he countered, shrugging. 'You are no longer a child to be protected from herself, my lovely wife.' He paused significantly. '*Inoltre*, you promised me only this morning that I would find you willing.'

'Well—yes. But not—not like this.' She swallowed desperately, realising that by some totally unscrupulous means he'd altered his position and was now lying beside her. Holding her. 'You seem to have forgotten that we—we're having dinner with your father,' she went on, improvising wildly. Realising, too, how absurd she must sound. 'I—I have to—get ready.'

'I have forgotten nothing, *carissima*.' Renzo's smile widened disgracefully into a grin of pure enjoyment at her stumbling words. 'Particularly your assurance that it will take you only five minutes to dress.'

He lifted a hand and brushed a strand of hair back from her flushed face. Ran an exploring finger down the curve of her cheek and across the moist heat of her startled, parted lips.

'So, at long last,' he added softly, 'we are together—and with all the time we need.'

CHAPTER NINE

MARISA stared up into the dark face poised above her, unable to think coherently. Scarcely able, she realised, to breathe. Shatteringly conscious of the heat of his lean body and the beguiling, never-forgotten scent of his skin: the clean tang of the soap he used overlaid with the faint musky fragrance of his cologne.

The almost hypnotic beat of his heart was imprinting itself on her spread hands, still trapped against the hair-roughened wall of his chest, and finding an echo throughout her entire bloodstream.

Then Renzo bent his head, and for only the second time in her life she felt the warmth of his mouth on hers. But not in the way she'd experienced in that brief contact this morning, she thought, her brain reeling. No—it was not like that at all.

Because this was an unhurried and totally deliberate exploration of the contours of her mouth, unlike anything she'd ever encountered before or expected to meet with. And although his lips were still gentle, they were also offering a frank enticement which she could not ignore. Or, it seemed, resist.

Not this time…

Then, in one dizzy, shaking moment, Marisa knew that her instincts had been entirely accurate. Understood completely why she'd been so right all this time to keep him at arm's length and further.

Why she'd reacted so violently to his touch on her wedding night—and later, when she'd been offered the chance of escape, why she'd fled across Europe, telling herself it was over.

Determined to make it so by doing her utmost to cut him completely out of her memory, her life.

And, God help me, she thought with anguish, *my heart*.

Renzo lifted his head and looked down at her for a long moment, before leaning down again to brush small kisses on her forehead, her half-closed eyes and along the betraying hectic flush that she could feel heating her cheekbones.

Then his mouth returned to hers with renewed urgency, and involuntarily, devastatingly, her lips were parting under his insistence, allowing the silken glide of his tongue to invade the inner moist heat that he sought.

She found too that she was no longer trying to push him away. That in fact she was not simply yielding to his kiss, but slowly and shyly offering him a response.

And that as a result his demand was deepening—turning to undisguised and passionate hunger.

When he lifted his head, they were both breathless.

His lambent gaze holding hers, Renzo ran a caressing finger along the curve of her lower lip.

'You are trembling, *mia bella*.' His voice was soft. 'Am I truly such an object of terror to you still?'

She stared back at him, wordlessly shaking her head. Not terror, she thought, but excitement and the promise of unimagined delight.

Everything that she most feared from him. Everything that she most desired.

He said, half to himself, 'And I came here only to talk…'

He drew her back to him. His lips touched her throat, dwelt for an instant on the leaping, uneven pulse, then found her ear, caressing its inner whorls with the tip of his tongue and allowing his teeth to graze softly at its small pink lobe, forcing a gasp from her.

His mouth moved downward, planting kisses on the delicate line of her neck before lingering in the fragrant hollow at its base.

She didn't even know when he'd slipped her bra straps from her shoulders, but they were certainly bare when he traced their slenderness with his lips, touching her skin as if it was fragile silk.

At the same time his fingertips began to glide gently over the exposed curves of her breasts, where they rose above the scalloped edge of her bra, and she felt her nipples swell and harden against their lace confinement in a response to his touch, which was as stark as it was involuntary.

His hand slid under her back, releasing the metal clasp so that he could slip the tiny garment from her body completely and allow his fingers to cup her breasts instead, stroking them gently, almost reverently, while his lips captured hers again, caressing them with an explicit insistence she was unable to refuse.

More than that, as she returned his kisses Marisa found she was touching him in turn, pushing his shirt from his shoulders in clumsy haste so that her eager, untutored hands could begin to learn his body. Could seek the muscled planes and angles of his shoulders and the supple length of his spine under the satiny skin.

Could turn his kiss, too, into a sigh of longing.

Renzo reached down and threw the shrouding coverlet aside, his hands drifting slowly and sweetly down the length of her body before returning to her tumescent breasts, taking them in the palms of his hands and offering them to the candid adoration of his mouth.

His lips gently possessed first one scented mound and then the other, his tongue teasing the puckered rosy peaks with lingering sensual expertise.

Her body was alive, quivering with the sensations he was provoking, and fierce shafts of delight were running through her like a flame in the blood as she arched towards him, stifling a little sob. Wanting more.

And—as his questing hand slid down over her ribcage and her stomach to the flimsy barrier of her briefs—wanting everything…

Only to feel his whole body grow suddenly tense,

and to realise that he was lifting himself away from her, looking across the room at the door, his brows snapping together.

Reality came storming back as she heard it too—the sound of knocking, followed by a woman's voice.

'What—who is it?' Her voice was unrecognisable.

Renzo called sharply in his own language, 'A moment, if you please.' He turned back to Marisa. 'It is Rosalia,' he told her ruefully, shrugging. 'The maid who attended you earlier. She has come to prepare your bath and assist you to change.' He added dryly, 'My father's orders, you understand.'

He paused, looking down at her. 'So, does she come in, *carissima*?' he asked softly. 'Or shall I send her away in order that I may bathe and dress you myself—later?'

But the spell was broken, and the flush that warmed her face was suddenly one of embarrassment—not just at the unexpected interruption, but at the intimate picture his words had conjured up.

Also at the realisation of how close she had come to absolute surrender. And not just of her body, but her mind and will too.

She said, stumbling a little, 'But if you tell her to go then she'll know that we're—together. And why…'

'As we are married,' he said levelly, 'it will hardly come as any great surprise to her.'

'Yes.' Her blush deepened. 'But she might—say something—to other people.'

'It could happen.' Renzo studied her wryly. 'I think,

mia bella, you must accustom yourself to a little curiosity from the staff. They too have waited a long time to see you here.'

'I understand that.' She snatched up her bra and fumbled it back into place, avoiding his gaze as she struggled with the hook. Telling herself to be thankful that matters had gone no further. 'But it's all too soon for me. I can't deal with it yet—this living under a spotlight. Knowing that everything that happens is going to be under scrutiny.'

Including, no doubt, the moment I become pregnant...

'Ah,' he said quietly. 'Then the answer to my question is no.'

He moved her hands aside, dealing briskly and deftly with the recalcitrant clip on her bra, then he lifted the soft mass of hair and dropped a kiss on the nape of her neck.

It was the lightest caress, but it made her burn and shiver all over again.

He said, 'I will leave you to your maid, Maria Lisa. But we still have to talk, *carissima.*' There was an odd note in his voice—almost strained. 'There are things that have to be said—things I think you must know— before we begin our real marriage.'

Retrieving his crumpled shirt, he swung himself off the bed and strode off towards his own room, leaving Marisa frantically hauling the coverlet back into place and straightening the pillows in an attempt to eliminate any indication of recent events.

Renzo paused in the doorway, sending her a final, frankly sardonic glance as he observed her efforts.

'Save yourself the trouble, *carissima*,' he advised. 'You would not deceive a blind woman.'

He called, *'Avanti*, Rosalia,' and disappeared, closing the door behind him.

The last thing in the world Marisa wanted was a personal maid, but Rosalia seemed quiet, and eager to please, discreetly ignoring her young employer's state of flushed dishevelment. But she was clearly distressed that the *signora* did not have a suitable dress in which to grace her father-in-law's celebration dinner table.

She listened with open astonishment to Marisa's halting explanation of mislaid luggage, her expression saying clearly that heads would roll at any airline foolish enough to mislay so much as a paper bag belonging to the Santangeli family.

In the end, it had to be the wrap-around skirt from the previous evening, teamed this time with a high-necked Victorian-style blouse in broderie anglaise. Not ideal, but the best she could do under the circumstances.

The circumstances…

She had to admit it was pleasant having a scented bath drawn and waiting for her, but the size of the deep, wide tub she was lying in, together with the twin washbasins and another of those king-size walk-in showers, its glass panels etched with flowers, all served to remind her that this bathroom had been specifically designed for dual occupation.

And that sharing this space with Renzo was yet another intimacy of marriage she would have to learn. And quickly.

What was more, she reflected as she dried herself, it was a space that had too many mirrors for her taste, with far too many naked Marisas reflected in them.

She gave the nearest image a fleeting glance, a hand straying to the curve of her breast as she remembered the other fingers that had touched it—the sensuous mouth that had brought the nipple to vibrant, aching life.

Recalled too the brief force of his body inside her own all those months ago. The moment when she'd realised she did not want his possession of her, however curt and perfunctory, to stop.

Acknowledged, without pride, that even the thought of it had caused her unfulfilled body to burn—to scald—with need ever since.

Which had always been an excellent reason for not thinking of it, she thought wryly as she rubbed body lotion in her favourite scent into her skin and put on fresh underwear.

But now, once again, as the events of the past half-hour had taught her, she had no choice. Because, as he'd proved in one succinct lesson, she could no longer pretend indifference to him.

It was not simply a matter of keeping the strictly

conditional promise she'd made him in London that morning. Not any more.

No longer a granting of permission to take what he wanted, but no more.

Nor a private but steely resolve that, no matter what he did, she would somehow maintain her stance of indifference. Hold herself aloof from any possibility of genuine intimacy between them.

That was no longer possible.

Because, for good or ill, she'd been brought here to live with him as his wife. And this time it was the whole package.

Although nothing had fundamentally changed, she reminded herself painfully. Renzo might have proved beyond doubt that he could arouse her to the point of no return—but then, after their past encounters, his pride would demand no less.

Our real marriage. Renzo's own words, she thought. But without love they were meaningless. Nothing more than an invitation to sexual satisfaction.

But it wasn't just his lovemaking that would hold her in thrall to him. It was this enforced proximity of everyday living that was the actual danger to her heart, just as it always had been.

Because she'd already undergone a crash course in the subject of Renzo Santangeli during her earlier time in this house, and she hadn't forgotten a thing.

Even before she'd discovered desire she'd learned to crave his company, judge his moods, bask in his kindness—and to feel only half-alive when he wasn't there.

The sound of his voice in the distance had always been enough to set her heart racing. But apart from that moment of supreme lunacy in the swimming pool, she'd always managed to hide all the myriad feelings she had for him. Even, for a long time, to pretend they did not exist.

But now she had to share these admittedly spacious rooms with him, when, apart from sex, all he'd ever offered her was friendship.

So she would have to be careful never to hint by word or gesture that she might want much more, because that could lead to another rejection. And that would be—unendurable.

These are the circumstances, she told herself. And somehow I have to abide by them.

And sighing, she walked back into her bedroom.

She'd planned to wear her hair loose, as usual, but the waiting Rosalia was quite adamant about transforming it into a skilfully casual topknot, with a few soft strands to frame the face.

It provided a distinct touch of elegance, she discovered when it was done, and Rosalia was smiling and nodding.

And heaven knows, Marisa thought, as she applied a touch of soft pink to her mouth, *I'm going to need all the help I can get this evening.*

She found herself wondering a little shyly if Renzo

would like her new style, but when he came to escort her downstairs, himself resplendent in a dark grey suit, his pristine white shirt set off by a deep crimson tie, he made no comment, seeming lost in his own thoughts. Nor were they particularly happy ones, if the grim set of his mouth was to be believed.

But what was wrong? Surely he couldn't be annoyed because she'd failed to send Rosalia away earlier? He must know that her surrender had only been postponed, not denied.

Perhaps he, too, was simply dreading tonight's dinner party.

Her premonition that this could be a seriously tricky occasion was reinforced into bleak certainty when she entered the *salotto* at his side and met Teresa Barzati's inimical gaze, directed at her from a high-backed chair at the side of the fireplace.

Impenetrably dark eyes swept her from head to foot, taking in every inch of the chainstore clothing, and the thin mouth pursed itself in open disapproval.

But what did it matter if she was inappropriately dressed when it came in the wake of so many other flaws? Marisa asked herself resignedly.

The *signora* herself clearly didn't do informal. Her own dress was black silk, its sombre magnificence relieved only by the matching emerald bracelets that adorned each bony wrist.

They were undoubtedly beautiful, and probably priceless, but Marisa found their brilliance oddly barbaric, and totally at odds with the general severity of the older woman's appearance.

'So you have decided to come back, Marisa,' was Nonna Teresa's eventual greeting, accompanied by a faint sniff. 'I suppose we must be gratified that you have at last remembered where your duty lies. And hope that you do not forget again.'

There was an appalled silence. As Marisa gasped, her face reddening with mingled indignation and embarrassment, Renzo's hand closed over hers.

He said softly, 'But my grandmother forgot to say, Maria Lisa, how delighted she is to see you again.' He looked at the older woman. 'Is that not so, Nonna?'

There was a pause, then Signora Barzati gave an abrupt jerk of the head that might have been interpreted as a nod.

Guillermo came surging forward at this juncture, offering Marisa an *aperitivo* and telling her pointedly how pretty she looked.

She was grateful, but hardly reassured, as she took a seat on one of the long sofas beside Ottavia Alesconi, chic in amethyst linen.

She'd hardly expected a full-frontal attack, she thought shakily. But clearly Renzo knew that his grandmother would be unable to resist some biting remark, and had been prepared for it.

Well, she'd done her worst, and now it was over, so perhaps they could all relax. Perhaps...

Yet when Emilio, her father-in-law's stately major-domo, eventually announced dinner, and although the food was delicious, as always, the atmosphere in the dining room was far from celebratory.

On the contrary, everyone seemed on edge still. Apart, that was, from Signora Barzati, who had commandeered the hostess's chair at the foot of the table—to Guillermo's open but silent annoyance—and was conducting a series of majestic monologues on the political situation, the iniquities of the taxation structure, plus the continued and unnecessary influx of foreign residents.

And no prizes for guessing who falls into that category, Marisa thought, trying to feel amused but not succeeding. She glanced across at Renzo, seated opposite, and realised he was already watching her, his mouth still unsmiling, but the golden eyes heavy with hunger. And something more. Something altogether less easy to define, she thought, as swift, shy heat invaded her face.

She would almost have said he was anxious—uncertain. But that was absurd, she told herself. After all, only a few hours before she'd betrayed herself utterly in his arms. And now she had nowhere left to hide. No more excuses to deny him the complete physical response he would soon demand from her.

When dinner ended, they were about to move back to the *salotto* for coffee, but Guillermo, who was looking tired, made his apologies and announced his intention to retire.

'Forgive me, my child.' He kissed Marisa on the forehead. 'We will talk together tomorrow.' He turned to Renzo. 'A word with you, my son? I promise I will not detain you too long from your wife's company.'

'My dear Guillermo.' Signora Barzati's tone was acid. 'You are joking, of course. After the events of the past year, that can hardly be an issue.'

'Basta!' He gave her a look of hauteur. 'I believed we had agreed to leave the past alone and look only to the future. I ask you, my dear mother-in-law, to remember that.'

She shrugged and turned away, walking into the *salotto* ahead of Marisa and Signora Alesconi, and resuming the seat she had occupied before the meal.

There was an awkward silence, rendered even more difficult when the coffee was brought in and the tray placed almost pointedly on a table beside Marisa. A move the *signora* observed with raised eyebrows and tightly compressed lips.

Then the door closed behind Emilio, and the three women were left alone.

By some miracle Marisa managed to pour coffee from the heavy pot without spillage or any other accident, and once they were all served Ottavia Alesconi immediately embarked on a flow of light, almost nervous chat, talking of a book she had just read, the coming opera season at Verona, and a new young designer who had taken Milan's fashion world by storm.

'Perhaps we should engage his services for

Marisa,' said Nonna Teresa coldly, when the younger woman paused. 'She is clearly in need of someone's guidance. Someone to explain to her that Santangeli wives do not dress like penniless schoolgirls.'

Ottavia Alesconi bit her lip. 'I think Signora Santangeli looks charming,' she said quietly.

'Charming?' The older woman gave a grating laugh. 'She will need much more than charm if she is to sustain Lorenzo's interest long enough for him to render her *incinta*.'

'Signora Barzati,' Ottavia protested, casting a shocked glance at Marisa's burning face. 'That is hardly a topic for discussion amongst us.'

'Because it is a matter that should be kept within the family?' The *signora* moved her hands and her bracelets glinted in the lamplight like the eyes of malevolent cats. 'But surely we can have no secrets from you, my dear Signora Alesconi? Now that my son-in-law has apparently installed you here in my late daughter's place. And while I cannot be expected to approve of such a situation,' she added silkily, 'at least you are a widow, with no husband in the background to create a scandal—unlike Lorenzo's present mistress.'

It was suddenly difficult to breathe. Marisa found that the lamplit room seemed to have receded suddenly to some immense distance. She put her coffee cup back on the table with extreme care, as if it might dissolve at her touch.

The only reality was the cold, scornful voice, speaking with perfect clarity as it flayed the skin from her bones.

'No doubt Doria Venucci's beauty, and other attributes, have convinced my grandson that their affair is worth the risk.' Her smile was pure acid. 'Small wonder, too, *cara* Marisa, that he has been in no hurry to recall you from England. It is only his pressing need for an heir that has restored you to us at all—as I am sure you know.'

'Yes,' Marisa said, in a voice she did not recognise. 'I—know.'

'But what I must ask myself,' Nonna Teresa went on softly, 'is if it is likely that a girl already more trouble than she is worth can prevent Lorenzo from pursuing this disgraceful liaison which could be the ruin of us all. For myself, I think not.'

Ottavia Alesconi was on her feet. 'Signora Barzati,' she said in a choked voice. 'I—I must protest.'

'You do not agree with me, Signora Alesconi?' The older woman sounded mildly interested. 'You are, of course, very much a woman of the world. Perhaps you can use your…experience in pleasing men to give Marisa some tips—advise her on ways to ensure that Lorenzo does his duty and spends his nights in her bed, where he belongs.

'Something she has signally failed to accomplish so far,' she added with contempt. 'And I hold out little hope for the future.'

'This is unpardonable, *signora*.' Ottavia Alesconi's

voice was ice. 'I overlook your insults to me—they are no more than I expected. But to turn your venom on an innocent girl—and at such a time—is beyond forgiveness.'

'Venom?' Nonna Teresa repeated. 'But you misunderstand, *signora*. I merely wish her to be under no illusion about the task ahead of her. To appreciate that once she is no longer a novelty for Lorenzo he will quickly become bored and look for other entertainment. If she is prepared for his—diversions, surely she is less likely to be hurt.'

'You are the one who does not understand, *signora*.'

She was dying inside, but somehow Marisa got to her feet and faced her adversary, her head high.

'You speak as if this was a love-match. As if Renzo and I—care for each other. But we do not, as everyone must be aware. You pointed out yourself that he married me only so that he could have a child—an heir.' She lifted her chin. 'It is a strictly limited commitment that suits us both perfectly. Therefore I do not need illusions, Signora Barzati. Nor do I expect fidelity. The fact that Renzo has other women does not matter to me. Why should it, when I don't love him?

'And once Renzo has his son, he is at liberty to choose any bed in the world—just so long as it isn't mine.'

She turned to the door and saw him standing there, silent and motionless, his face that of a stranger, carved from stone. The golden eyes blank with disbelief.

She had no idea how long he'd been in the doorway. How much he'd heard. But it had surely been enough.

A slow knife turned inside her, and she could have screamed with the pain of it. Could have stormed and wept and begged him to pretend—to lie that there was no one else. That for this one brief time he would be hers alone.

But she could not embarrass him—or herself—in such a way. Could not betray her inner agony.

Instead, keeping her voice cool and level, she said, 'Perhaps you would confirm for your grandmother, *signore*, the practicalities of our arrangement, and assure her that her kind advice, however well meant, is quite unnecessary?'

She added quietly, 'Forgive me if I do not stay, but it has been a long and tiring day. I would therefore prefer not to be disturbed—under the circumstances. I am sure you understand.'

And she went past him, her bright tearless eyes staring into space. Back to the lonely rooms and the empty bed waiting for her upstairs.

CHAPTER TEN

MARISA had not known it was possible to hurt so much and feel so empty at the same time. As if she'd been hollowed out and left to bleed.

She'd claimed tiredness, but she turned back at her bedroom door, knowing that she couldn't yet lie down on the bed where only a few hours ago she'd been held in Renzo's arms, her whole body alive and eager with the promise of joy.

But that was the illusion, she thought, shivering. Imagining even for a moment that she could exist on sex alone. Or his offer of friendship. That she could somehow make them enough when she wanted so much more. When she wanted—everything.

And now, in a few corrosive, malignant minutes, the impossibility of that had been spelled out to her in terms that left no room for hope.

That told her she was worse than a fool to think that Renzo's lovemaking could be prompted by anything but expediency. That he'd decided having her warm and responsive in his bed would simply make his task easier. And then, his duty accomplished, he would return to the glamorous forbidden mistress who'd kept him in Rome all this time, his marriage sidelined once again—for her sake.

So, for a while, she thought with pain, she didn't want to go back to that room—that bed. She needed quite badly to be…somewhere else.

Slowly, her arms wrapped round her body, she went along to the room at the end of the passage. On her previous visit it had been turned into another *salotto*—their own private sitting room. With a television, and a sophisticated sound system for Renzo's music collection and an alcove for dining.

Now it was long finished, the walls painted a restful colour between pale gold and apricot, and the shuttered windows that gave access to the *loggia* overlooking the garden hung with curtains in plain bleached linen.

The same fabric had been used to upholster the large, thickly cushioned sofa in front of the fireplace, and after lighting one of the tall lamps Marisa curled herself into one capacious corner, feeling the quiet comfort of the place close round her and wishing it could absorb her completely. That she could just…vanish, and never be seen again.

Never have to face anyone or try to deal with the wasteland her life had become.

Now, too late, she could understand the strange atmosphere she'd sensed in the house. It had been the uneasy calm before the storm. Because they must all have feared that Teresa Barzati had come there only to cause trouble.

I was the only one who didn't realise, she thought.

And while Zio Guillermo's reproof to the *signora* had provided a momentary respite, it had failed to silence her in the real mischief she planned to make. But then nothing could have done that.

Zia Maria, she thought bleakly, remembering her godmother's laughing eyes and the warm, comforting arms. Always there for her. How could all that gentleness possibly have been born from such hating and bitterness? From a hostility that had chilled her from the first?

Not that she'd been the only target tonight, she reminded herself. Ottavia Alesconi had also suffered from the *signora*'s malice. But in the scale of things Ottavia had got off lightly.

The real, lasting brutality had been aimed unerringly at herself.

Doria Venucci. She tried the name under her breath. A woman beautiful—experienced—and married. Everything she'd needed to know in one smiling, destructive sentence.

And everything that she was not, she thought, remembering those endless mirrors in the bathroom.

Because she was nothing special and never had been. Her sole venture into allure had been a disaster, whatever Renzo might have told her earlier, when he was trying to seduce her.

Although I have novelty value, she thought, digging her nails into the palms of her hands. *Let's not forget that.*

Or that for a few brief moments he almost made me forget something—the reason I'm here. The only reason...

She would not, however, allow herself to cry. That was definitely not an option. Because she needed to stay calm and rational in order to prepare for the moment when she would have to face Renzo again. When all her skill at self-protection would be brought into play once more.

Because wasn't that what the whole of the past year had really been about? Mounting guard on her emotions—her needs? Denying every instinct—every desire?

Nothing but an endless, futile attempt to convince herself that the war going on inside her was really fuelled by hate, she told herself broodingly. At the same time armouring herself against the possibility that one day he might come back.

And what good had it done her? she asked herself with despair. It had only taken a few kisses—the stroke of his hand on her breast—to bring her conquered and whimpering into his arms.

But for Rosalia's intervention she would have committed the worst mistake of her life—would have given herself completely—and she knew it. And in her surrender could have betrayed herself irretrievably. Could have sobbed out her pathetic yearnings against his skin.

Might even have broken the ultimate taboo and said the 'love' word, she thought in self-derision. At least she'd been spared that.

Otherwise, after tonight's bombshell had exploded, she'd have been forced to live, humiliated beyond belief, with the consequences of her own folly.

But now she needed to be strong. So a tear-stained face would simply be a sign of weakness she could not afford.

She moved restlessly, wondering what was happening in the other part of the house. What kind of recriminations were being aired.

No doubt she would find out tomorrow, she thought, then realised, with a startled glance at her watch, that it was nearly the next day already.

And that, in spite of her reluctance, it was time she went to bed.

I need to do the rational—the conventional thing, she told herself. As if it had been just another evening, and the *signora* had only been giving her some kindly but misguided advice.

A little tactless, maybe, but no lasting damage done.

Yes, that would be the way to handle it in the morning. As if the older woman's poisonous revelations really didn't matter.

With never a hint that she was falling to pieces and might never be whole again.

* * *

Rosalia seemed to have been busy again, because Marisa found her bed had been turned down—on both sides—and her nightgown arranged prettily on the coverlet.

She's clearly an optimist, Marisa thought ironically as she undressed quickly and slipped the white voile folds over her head. *Or maybe, if there's any kind of furore going on downstairs, it hasn't reached the servants' quarters yet.*

She went through the routine of removing her make-up, before finally unpinning her hair and brushing it loose into a silky cloud on her shoulders.

Then she walked reluctantly over to the bed, climbed in, and turned to switch off the lamp.

Only to realise with sudden, frozen shock that she was no longer alone. That Renzo was there, standing silently in the open doorway of his room.

'So,' he said at last, 'you are not asleep, after all.'

'But I plan to be,' she said tautly. 'In about two minutes.'

He was wearing, she noticed, one of the white towelling robes hanging in the bathroom and almost certainly nothing else. She felt her mouth go dry.

'And I thought I asked to be left in peace,' she added with hauteur.

'Is that how you see the present situation?' he asked. 'As peaceful?' His mouth twisted. 'You astonish me, *mia cara*.'

She bit her lip. 'But then in some ways it's been

quite an astonishing evening all round, *signore*.' She
made a business of arranging her pillows. 'Now,
perhaps you'll excuse me?'

'There is nothing to excuse.' He came across to the
bed and sat down on its edge, looking at her. 'You
have taken down your hair,' he commented meditatively. 'I had hoped to do that for myself.' He smiled
at her. 'Before, of course, I removed the charming
concealment of that blouse, and everything else you
were wearing tonight.'

'You—hoped?' Marisa echoed, her throat tightening to choking point.

She mustered her resources. 'How—how dare you?
Just—get out of here.'

He smiled faintly. 'I grieve to disappoint you, Maria
Lisa, but I am going nowhere.'

She stared at him. 'Is this some kind of sick joke?'
she asked unsteadily. 'Because, arrogant as you are,
you can't possibly imagine you're going to stay here.
That I would allow you to—to…'

'But it has always been my intention to share your
bed, *mia cara sposa*.' His gaze was steady. 'To make
this the wedding night we never had. And nothing has
happened to change my mind.'

'Nothing?' Marisa queried hoarsely. 'My God,
didn't I make it clear enough that you wouldn't be
welcome?'

'As always, you were a model of clarity, *mia
bella*. Even my grandmother was left with nothing

to say. And that does not happen very often,' he added reflectively.

He paused. 'You may be relieved to learn that she will be leaving after breakfast, and that any future visits will be—discouraged.'

'Why? Because she told the truth?' She took a quick harsh breath. 'Or are you now going to deny that you've been having an affair?'

'Deny it?' His brows lifted. 'Why should I?'

She stared at him defiantly. 'That underworked sense of decency you once mentioned, perhaps?'

'But I prefer to begin our marriage with honesty, Maria Lisa, rather than a convenient lie,' Renzo retorted. 'In spite of my efforts you were clearly determined to prolong your absence from me. To behave, in fact, as if I had ceased to exist for you.'

'I hoped you had,' she threw back recklessly.

'I do not doubt it.' His voice hardened. 'But did you really expect me to live like a eunuch until you chose or were forced to return?'

She gasped. 'You really have no sense of shame, do you?'

'An overrated virtue, I think.' He shrugged. 'Although I admit I deeply regret that I was stupid enough to seek consolation when you shut me out of your life, rather than take a more effective course of action. I must learn to curb my temper.'

He went on flatly, 'I also wish very much that I had done as I planned this evening and told you about the affair myself, before anyone else had a chance to do so.'

She stared at him. 'You—planned?' Her voice sounded dazed.

'*Sì*. I told you when I visited you earlier that there were things that needed to be said between us. But then I allowed myself to be—most exquisitely— diverted from my purpose,' he added ruefully. 'I hoped there would be time later, but unfortunately my grandmother always likes to be the first with bad news, so I had no chance to talk to you…to explain, perhaps, how—why—it happened.

'In that Nonna Teresa bears a certain resemblance to your cousin Julia,' he added coldly. 'We are neither of us blessed with our relatives, *carissima*.'

'You may think that.' Marisa lifted her chin. 'On the other hand, I shall always be grateful to them both, for reminding me what you're really like—and the kind of life I might expect with you.' She took a breath. 'Besides, what was there for you to explain— apart from the fact that you're a—a serial womaniser who can't keep his zip fastened?'

There was a tingling silence.

'Never a problem when I was near you, my little saint,' Renzo returned eventually, and too courteously. 'Although even you are not immune to the temptations of the flesh with other men, it seems.'

She gasped. 'What the hell do you mean?'

'Those intimate lunches with the unhappy hus-

band,' he came back at her. 'Where might they ultimately have led, if he had asked for more than
sympathy? Also the unfortunate Alan, who accompanied you back to your cosy flat with its one bed only
last night, *mia sposa.*' The golden eyes narrowed.
'What would have happened, I wonder, if I had not
been so tactlessly waiting?'

'Nothing,' she said curtly.

'How can you be so sure?'

Because I've never loved anyone but you, she
thought, staring down at the coverlet. *Never loved or
wanted any other man. That's the truth I've had to
hide ever since you walked back into my life and
asked me to marry you. That's the truth I've been
trying to hide from myself all this time.*

*Because you don't feel the same, and you never
will. You only want someone to give you a child and
turn a blind eye to your other women.*

*And I—I want all the things you can't give me. I
want all of you, and that's what makes any real
honesty between us impossible.*

*Because I couldn't bear it—I'd die before I let you
find out how I really feel and embarrass you or have
you feel sorry for me.*

Aloud, she said shortly, 'Alan blew his chances
when he took the money and ran off to Hong Kong.'
She swallowed. 'But even if I had planned to take a
lover, what possible right would you have to object
when you have a mistress?'

'I have whatever rights I choose,' Renzo retorted crisply. 'And one is to ensure that I have you first, *carissima*. So that I can be certain that any child in your body will be mine and no other's.'

As she gasped in outrage, he paused. 'Also, my grandmother is out of date. The affair with Doria Venucci is already over,' he added, with a touch of grimness. 'And for that you have my word.'

'To spare my feelings?' she asked defiantly. 'Or to avoid the scandal your grandmother was predicting tonight?'

'Oh, the scandal, *naturalamente*.' His voice bit. 'I was not aware you had any feelings about our marriage—apart from resentment and distaste. But the gossipmongers were at work long before I met Signora Venucci—theorising on the reasons for our prolonged separation,' he added broodingly. 'Do not imagine I found their speculation pleasant.'

'Oh, how terrible for you,' she flung back at him. 'I never realised you were so sensitive, *signore*.'

'No,' he said harshly. 'That I can also believe.' He paused. 'Tell me something, *mia cara*, *per favore*. Just as you never returned any of my phone calls, did you ever read even one of the letters I wrote to you?'

She hadn't been expecting that. Had tried to put out of her mind the airmail envelopes, which had arrived so regularly, only to be torn up and binned, unopened.

She didn't particularly want to confess the awkward truth, but realised she couldn't sustain a lie either. He would be bound to ask questions about their contents that she'd be unable to answer.

She played with the edge of the embroidered sheet. 'No,' she admitted eventually. 'No, I didn't.'

'Che peccato,' he said. 'What a pity. You might have found them—instructive.'

She said defiantly, 'Or perhaps I felt I'd already learned what I needed to know about you, *signore*.'

He said silkily, 'But as you discovered in this room a few hours ago, *signora*, your lessons are only just beginning.' And he began to loosen the belt of his robe.

Marisa hurled herself on to her side, turning her back to him. Because she couldn't see him naked— she *dared* not...

'No,' she said hoarsely. 'Do you think saying your affair is over makes everything all right? Signora Venucci wasn't the first, *signore*, and she won't be the last. Knowing that, do you really think I'm going to allow you anywhere near me again?'

She felt the mattress dip slightly as he joined her in the bed, and her whole body tensed.

'Why, yes.' His voice reached her softly. 'Because that is what you agreed to do. In return, if you remember, for living the rest of your life in whatever way you wish. The agreement we reached only this morning. And also because you don't love me, Maria Lisa,' he went on. 'Nor are you in the least concerned if there are other women in my life, because you are only here to have my baby.'

He paused. 'You said so yourself, if you remember. Not long ago, and in front of witnesses too.'

His hand touched her bare shoulder. Stroked its soft skin with heart-stopping gentleness. 'So, if you don't care what I do, *mia cara*, if you are so supremely indifferent to the way I live my life and how I amuse myself when you are not there, why should it matter to you whether Doria Venucci goes or stays? Or who might take her place?

'Therefore what possible excuse do you have to withhold yourself from me any longer. To refuse to behave as my wife—and the future mother of my son? When this, on your own admission, is your sole consideration.'

Marisa could not speak or move. It occurred to her suddenly that this was how a hunted animal must feel when the trap closed around it. But this was a trap entirely of her own making.

But I do care, she cried out soundlessly. *Oh, God, I care so much.*

Just the thought of you with another woman is like a giant claw ripping into me. Tearing me apart. Making me only half a human being. Only I can never tell you so. I have to go on pretending.

Aloud, she said very quietly, 'I suppose—logically—I have no excuse.'

'*Bene,*' Renzo approved, his tone ironic. 'At last we have reached an understanding. Tonight we will put the past behind us for ever, and you will learn to belong to me completely. And do not think to escape by telling me to do my worst,' he added mockingly. 'We have already trodden that path, and I found it—unrewarding.'

She said unevenly, 'You—bastard.'

'And no insult will stop me either,' Renzo retorted. 'You see, my reluctant wife, there was something about your latest piece of candour that intrigued me. While you were proclaiming your indifference you may have denied love, but you failed to mention—desire.'

His voice sank to a whisper. 'You never said, *carissima*, that you did not want me. Maybe because you knew it was not true, as you proved earlier right here in this room. Or did you think I had forgotten how sweet you were—how yielding?'

He allowed his words to settle into a tingling silence, then his hands closed on her, turning her inexorably to face him.

'So, for tonight at least, Maria Lisa, listen to your body, not your mind.'

Oh, God, he only has to touch me and I'm trembling inside—going to pieces...

'I'll give you nothing.' Her voice shook.

'You intend to break your word to me?' Renzo tutted in faint reproof as he tossed the covers away to the foot of the bed. 'I do not recommend it, *mia bella*.' He added meditatively, 'Also, I wonder if you can.'

He looked at the thin layer of voile that masked her body and smiled slowly. 'And now it seems that I have the privilege of undressing you just a little after all.'

'No.' She pushed at the hands that were drawing the straps of her nightgown down from her shoulders. 'I—I'll keep my promise—but…don't…please…'

'You wish to do it for me?' he asked, and his smile became a teasing, almost wicked grin. 'Even better. Having you strip for me has always been one of my favourite fantasies,' he added huskily. 'I am sure you remember why.'

Marisa turned her head away, her face warming helplessly, aware that just one unwanted glimpse of his lean, burnished body stretched against the snowy bedlinen had prompted the unwelcome resurrection of some of her own fantasies.

She said tautly, 'Do you have to—humiliate me like this?'

Reminding me how long I've loved you, how much I've always wanted to be yours—even when I could only guess…imagine… what that might mean?

'That is not my intention,' he said, with a sudden touch of harshness.

'But for once in our lives, Maria Lisa, I want there to be nothing to separate us from each other. Not clothing, not lies, not silence. Just a man with his wife.'

Her voice pleaded. 'Then will you at least let me turn out the light?'

'No,' he said. 'I will not.' He added more gently, '*Carissima*, I have waited so very long to see you— to hold you like this.'

She closed her eyes, trying to shut him out of her

consciousness. To deny what was happening between them. But her other senses were still only too alive, and she felt the fabric whisper against her skin as he discarded it. And in the silence that followed she heard him sigh quietly, and with undisguised satisfaction.

Then he reached for her, drawing her into his arms, making her aware of every inch of his undisguisedly urgent body against her nakedness as his lips took hers.

And while she could never accuse him of using force, nevertheless his kiss was deep—and, she discovered, also implacably, unrelentingly thorough. Sparing her nothing as it possessed her.

A declaration, she realised dazedly, of intent.

A challenge to her powers of resistance, stating silently but potently that it was useless for her to pretend she was unmoved by what he was doing to her.

And perhaps it was. But that didn't mean she had to add to her earlier mistakes by making it easy for him, or by adding her name to the list of eagerly compliant women who'd shared his bed, she told herself with a kind of ragged determination, keeping her eyes so tightly shut they began to ache.

But Renzo wasn't making it easy for her either, as his mouth continued to move achingly, intensely on hers.

As she was made to discover the heated excitement that the deliberately sensuous brush of his bare skin against hers could generate. And was reminded, as he pulled her even closer to his hard

loins, exactly how it had once felt to have all that
aroused male potency and strength sheathed deep
inside her.

And how, for one brief second of time, she had
wanted it to last for ever.

Yet giving herself now would make her all too vul-
nerable to discovery, she thought, clinging to her last
shreds of reason. Could lure her into betraying that
she had more at stake from this encounter than any
mere initiation into the deep waters of sensuality.

And if pride, maybe, and an atom of self-respect
might be all she could salvage from this welter of
confusion and unhappiness that was threatening to
overwhelm her, then she would settle for that.

Yet how could she battle her own needs when his
hands were renewing their lingering, pleasurable exploration of her body, tracing her bone structure as if
he wished to commit it to memory and gently
moulding every delicate curve and hollow?

When, wherever she felt his touch, her skin warmed
and blossomed in helpless pleasure, making her
senses swim?

She felt him lift his head and knew that he was
looking down at her. She was glad that he could not
see her eyes as his fingertips stroked her breasts,
coaxing the rosy nipples to aching, unresisting life,
making them stand proud for the homage of his lips.

And as they touched her—as she found herself
pierced by a pleasure that bordered pain—Marisa turned

her head away, pressing a clenched fist against the swollen contours of her mouth, biting at the knuckle.

This isn't making love, she thought desperately. *He's just testing your will—your capacity for endurance. So, fight. Fight, damn you. Don't let him know— don't ever let him see. You can't...*

Renzo's mouth enclosed each tumescent peak in turn, suckling them languorously, teasing them softly, exquisitely with his tongue. His fingers slowly traversed the flatness of her stomach, to outline the angle of one slender hip and close on it in a gesture so frankly proprietorial that she almost flinched.

Again she felt him pause, as if sensing—even gauging—her resistance, and his hand came up to capture her averted chin, compelling her to face him again.

She felt him smooth the hair back from her forehead, then brush a soft caress across her inimically closed eyelids, before returning to her mouth. And as he kissed her Marisa could taste the scent of her own skin on his lips.

His hands were moving again, sliding round to her back, his fingertips unhurriedly stroking the shivering skin up to her shoulderblades, then back down the graceful length of her spine to the sensitive area at its base, massaging it gently, before slipping down to caress the slight swell of her buttocks, his touch gentle, but deliberately inciting.

And for a shocked instant, in spite of herself,

Marisa found her body arching towards him in shivering response, feeling his dark chest hair graze her swollen nipples in a torment that was as delicious as it was calculated.

'*Carissima.*' She could feel his smile whispering the words against her mouth. '*Tesoro mio.*'

He shifted his position slightly, putting her back against the heaped pillows as he bent to her, kissing her throat, her shoulders and slender arms, while his fingers travelled down to the hollow of her hipbone and lingered there.

Marisa could feel the dark headlong rush of desire scalding her body as his hand descended slowly to seek the silky mound at the junction of her thighs, his touch like gossamer against the downy flesh. Persuading her, she realised, to open herself to the ultimate intimacies.

Realised too that her resistance was ebbing under the insidious pressure of this skilful, studied arousal.

That all the deep, hot places of her womanhood were melting in this musky, wanton surge of passion, yearning to offer up their secrets to his possession. And that Renzo would already know this. Would know exactly—oh, God—how to slide his hand between her slackened thighs and caress her moist inner flesh. How to find that tiny hidden nub that was somehow the centre of all delight and coax it to swell and harden under the delicate, practised play of his fingers as they stroked, circled and tantalised, just as her nipples were doing under the renewed cajolery of his tongue.

And Marisa was lost. She couldn't think or reason any more. Nothing seemed to exist but the sweet, terrifying anguish of this assault on her senses. The response that was being wrung from her shaken, defenceless body.

Her body was beginning to writhe, her hips lifting against his questing hand in mute pleading for—what?

For him to stop—to somehow end this shameful pleasure? To release her from this rack of delicious sensuality?

Or for him never to stop?

Her head turned restlessly on the pillows as she tried to stifle the moan of longing rising in her throat. The sound that would betray her utterly—telling him without words how desperately she needed to feel him inside her again. To feel him filling her, and offering the completion that had been denied when he'd taken her before.

And Renzo was whispering to her, his breath fanning her ear, his voice slurred and heavy as he told her that she was beautiful—that she was all the sweetness of the world—and, yes, it would be soon. It would be everything...

And in that moment she felt it, that first faint stirring deep within her, as if she was being drawn out of herself towards some distant unknown peak, with every nerve ending, every drop of blood concentrated, blindly focussed on that small, rapturous centre of sensation, aching and erect under the subtle, relentless glide of his fingertips.

Then, between one breath and the next, Marisa found herself overtaken, her shuddering, gasping body consumed by pulsations of pleasure spreading through every vein, every bone, every inch of her heated, shivering skin, each one more intense than the last. Until at their highest and fiercest pitch she thought she might faint or die, and heard herself cry out, her voice ragged with fear and wonder.

And when the hot, incredible trembling at last began to subside, she found herself wrapped closely in Renzo's arms, her sweat-dampened face buried in his shoulder and his lips against her hair.

Ashamed that, after all, she'd rendered him such an easy victory, but knowing that even if she wanted to she did not possess the strength to move away.

And that she did not want to…

CHAPTER ELEVEN

BUT at last it was Renzo who moved, reaching over the edge of the bed for his discarded robe.

Her body still quivering softly, Marisa opened weighted eyelids and stared at him, feeling suddenly bereft. Surely, surely that could not be all? a voice inside her begged. There must be more. There *had* to be…

Aloud, she said huskily, 'Where are you going?'

'Nowhere, *dolcezza mia.*' The reply was soft—almost soothing. When he turned back to her she realised he was tearing open a small packet taken from his pocket, and swiftly and deftly making use of its contents.

And in some dazed corner of her mind she thought, *But that can't happen. He shouldn't be doing that. Not if we're going to…*

Then he was drawing her once again into his arms, his mouth opening hers to admit the heated glide of his tongue. His hands stroked the length of her glowing body, then slid beneath her, lifting her towards the hardness of him that had already parted her unresisting thighs. He entered her with one sure, powerful thrust.

And all thought of protest died for her. Because, defying logic, reason and even common sense, this glorious and all-consuming sensation was what she'd been living for all these long, sterile months.

In spite of its comparative inexperience, her body, still blissfully euphoric in the wake of her first orgasm, was too relaxed to offer any impediment to his possession and she accepted him—welcomed him into her with joy.

It was so different, she thought, her mind reeling. So utterly—wonderfully different from that first time. Yet how could it possibly seem so right when everything between them was still so terribly wrong? And always would be...

And then, as Renzo began to move inside her, she abandoned all pretence at rationality and let her body think for her instead.

'I don't hurt you?' The question seemed torn from him as he looked down at her, the golden eyes searching hers. 'Maria Lisa—tell me—promise me that I do not...'

'No.' She breathed her answer, an instinct she'd not known she possessed prompting her to raise her hands and clasp his shoulders, to move her hips in slow, deliberate allurement. The ultimate physical reassurance—the candid offering of her entire self for his enjoyment.

At his instant, fervent reaction she closed on him hungrily, drawing him into her without reserve, holding him, then giving him release so that he could drive forward again, slowly and rhythmically, each time penetrating her more deeply, and surprising her into a gasp of raw pleasure.

Oh, God, he felt so amazing—so incredibly, dangerously beautiful...

At the same time her intuition told her that Renzo had himself well under control, patiently reining back his own needs in order to allow their bodies to became fully attuned to each other.

Until she realised her own responses, her own demands, should fully match his own, and they were finally joined in a harmony as old as the stars.

And even though she told herself it was—it must be—too soon, she could already feel within her, like a ripple on a tranquil sea, the renewed, irresistible build of helpless sexual excitement.

Felt it, reached for it, strained after it, half ashamed of her own greed, a tiny, frantic sob rising in her throat.

And in the next instant she found herself totally overwhelmed once more, her body throbbing in the harsh, almost feral throes of ecstasy as she moaned her pleasure aloud.

She became aware of Renzo rearing up above her, his head thrown back, throat muscles taut, as he gave a hoarse cry of rapture and his body shuddered into hers with the force of his own fulfilment.

Afterwards they lay motionless, still entwined, the only sound their ragged breathing as they struggled to return it to normality.

Marisa lay, eyes half-closed, her body still lost in its exquisite lassitude. She thought drowsily, *I'm not the same person, not any more. I've been transformed.*

She looked down tenderly at the dark head pillowed on her breasts, longing to hold him there for ever, to stroke his dishevelled hair, to kiss his eyes and mouth and whisper everything that her heart was crying out to tell him.

But she did not dare.

Because her mind was slowly and gradually beginning once more to deal with reality. Making her face a few essential truths.

Because nothing had changed at all. Not herself. And certainly not the situation that she was in.

Because sex, however magical, made no actual difference. And she must never fool herself into believing that it might.

So she did not try to stop him when eventually he eased himself away from her and left the bed to cross to the bathroom, but lay quietly, staring into space.

Asking herself how many more nights like this she could possibly endure. How deeply enmeshed in this web of passion and desire he'd spun round her might she become before she committed the cardinal sin of telling him that she loved him?

Might he even become so essential to her that there would come a time when she would not want to leave? A time when she would sacrifice every hope for the future and choose instead to remain here in his house, the obedient, docile wife, performing the domestic duties he'd outlined so succinctly to her only last night?

Careful never to be too curious about his absences. Scrupulous about ignoring the inevitable gossip that would reach her whenever he strayed too openly. And grateful for the occasional night when he would turn to her for his amusement.

Was it worth submitting to that kind of heartbreak? she asked herself wretchedly. Could she bear to watch herself slowly disintegrate in hurt and loneliness in this half-life he'd offered her?

No, she thought, shivering. *I—I can't do that. I won't...*

She made herself move, retrieve the covers from the foot of the bed and pull them into place, sheltering under them just before Renzo, yawning, came sauntering back into the room.

His brows lifted when he saw the straightened bed, but he made no comment as he slid in beside her, pulling her into his arms.

'Why don't we get a little sleep, *carissima*?' he suggested softly. 'Then see what the rest of the night brings.'

Novelty value...

The words seemed to beat in her head.

'No,' she said, taking a deep breath. 'I'd prefer not to.'

'You don't need to sleep?' Renzo whistled softly. 'You have miraculous powers of resilience, *mia cara*.

I wish I shared them, but being only a man,' he added ruefully, 'I need a little time to recover.'

'I meant,' she said thickly, 'I'd rather be alone.'

There was a fractional pause, then he said gently, 'But sleeping and waking together is all part of marriage, Maria Lisa.'

'For other people, perhaps. Not for us.'

Renzo released her, lifting himself on to an elbow as he stared down at her. 'What are you saying? Have I displeased you in some way?'

'I want to know why you did that,' she said hoarsely. 'Why you used—that thing when you're supposed to be making me pregnant.'

'Ah,' Renzo said softly. 'I understand. But there is plenty of time ahead of us for that, *cara mia*.' He stroked the curve of her cheek. 'And maybe we should learn to be husband and wife before we attempt to become father and mother.' He grinned reminiscently. 'My grandfather, Nonno Santangeli, had a saying— *First the pleasure in bed, later the joy in the cradle*.' He added softly, 'After what we have just shared I thought you might agree with him.'

'But I don't. My recollection of the agreement between us is quite different.' She swallowed past the unbearable tightness in her throat. 'You seem to have forgotten that I'm here for one purpose only, *signore*, and not as your—plaything.' She added flatly, 'You have—someone else for that.'

'*Dio mio*, not that again.' His mouth tightened. 'I

have told you—it is over. And it should never have begun, except...' He paused. 'Well, that does not matter. My concern is that you should believe me—and try, if you can, to forgive.' He added wryly, 'Or do you mean to punish me for the rest of our lives?'

'Signora Venucci may have been sidelined,' Marisa returned icily.

'But I'm sure there are plenty of other candidates waiting to take her place. Only I'm not one of them. I'm looking forward to my independence, and I won't be cheated out of it for a day longer than necessary just so that you can change the terms of our deal and use me as a substitute mistress.'

I can't believe I'm doing this—that I'm lying to him, saying these vile things, when every word is like sticking a knife into my own flesh.

'You believe that is what has happened here?' His voice changed—became harsh, almost derisive. 'My recollection is rather different. I think we *used* each other, Maria Lisa, and perhaps you cannot forgive me for that either. For showing you at last what your body was made for.'

'*Mille grazie,*' she said. 'It's always good to be taught by an expert.' She paused. 'No matter how that expertise was obtained. And by demonstrating that you can make me—amenable, you've mended your damaged pride in the process. Congratulations, *signore*. Everything's worked out for you.'

'I am glad you think so.' There was a silence, then

he added with a kind of terrible weariness, 'How can this be? How can I be apart from you for minutes, no more, yet find a different girl—this stranger—on my return?' He shook his head in bitter disbelief. '*Santa Madonna*, how can I be in heaven at one moment and hell the next?'

'Because you forgot why you married me,' she said, struggling to keep her voice level. Unemotional. 'Why you forced me to come back to you. But I haven't. And until you remember the terms of our agreement and decide to follow them, maybe you should spend your nights in your own room.'

'I have an even better suggestion,' he said with icy savagery. 'Why, *signora*, do you not simply provide me with a list of the days each month when you are most likely to conceive, so that I can restrict my visits to those occasions only?' He paused. 'In that way we will both be saved time and trouble.'

He flung back the covers and got up, reaching for his robe and shrugging it on.

As he fastened the belt, he looked down at her. 'You accused me of cheating you, Maria Lisa,' he said quietly. 'But I say you are the cheat—because you are deliberately denying yourself warmth and passion. Turning your back on the sweetness we could make together.'

She looked past him. Kept her voice cool. 'I'll survive.'

Will I? Can I? When I already feel as if I'm frag-

menting—breaking into tiny pieces. That I'll never be whole and entire again without you...

'And so shall I,' he said. 'As you say, there are plenty of other women in the world. Maybe I will find one who does not drive quite so hard a bargain. Who may even wish to be with me for myself.' His mouth twisted. 'But no doubt I am asking for the moon.'

And he turned away, walking across to his own room and closing the door behind him.

She nearly went after him. Nearly followed to tell him that she hadn't meant it—any of it. To beg him to come back. To hold her close and keep her safe. And to be there—at her side always.

Except that wasn't on offer.

There was sex, of course. The master with his latest pupil. He'd probably been sufficiently intrigued by the frenzy of her response to continue her lessons if she asked.

But how could she settle for a single course when she wanted an entire meal? A feast...?

And eventually there would be compensation, she thought achingly. A permissible focus for all the love dammed up in her heart, and one that she could even acknowledge, as she'd recognised that far-off day in the *piazza* at Amalfi.

There would be his baby...

So she could hope—live for that instead. Because, she thought, as she turned over, burying her unhappy face in the pillow that he'd used, trying to find some faint trace of him, because she had no other choice.

The Puccini aria with its theme of doomed love came to its plangent end.

She should, Marisa thought, get up and choose another CD—one, maybe, without quite so many resonances. But she remained where she was, curled up once more in the corner of the sofa in her private *salotto*.

Since she'd first arrived at the Villa Proserpina, three weeks earlier, the weather had remained unsettled, a mixture of sun and showers, with an occasional hint of thunder.

More in tune with her mood than brilliant heat, but hardly conducive to spending her afternoons in the garden or by the pool, so she was glad of this room as a kind of sanctuary.

At first she'd taken care to spend part of every day with her father-in-law, but now he'd begun to work in his study again, with his consultant's wary permission, preparing to pick up the reins at the bank once more.

'I hope he isn't overdoing things,' Marisa had said anxiously one evening after dinner, finding herself alone with Ottavia Alesconi, whose answering smile had been reassuring.

'Better, I think, that he should work a little than chafe at his restrictions.' She'd added meditatively, 'Also, it is necessary for him to take an interest as Lorenzo is away so much.'

Leaving Marisa to murmur an embarrassed, 'Yes—of course,' and hastily change the subject.

Because the truth was he was never there. In fact, she'd hardly set eyes on him since the night of their quarrel, she acknowledged wretchedly.

When she'd ventured downstairs the following morning, after a miserably restless night, it had been to discover that he'd already left for an appointment in Siena.

'You could have gone with him, dear child, but he insisted you should be left to sleep,' Guillermo had added, smiling, totally misinterpreting both Renzo's apparent solicitude and the deep shadows under her eyes.

He sees what he wants to see, Marisa had thought, stifling a sigh.

And when she and Renzo had met at dinner, the cool polite stranger of their honeymoon had returned. So much so that Marisa had wondered whether she'd only dreamed the events of the previous night. Because there was surely no way in which she could ever have sobbed the rapture of her climax in this man's arms.

Later, she had waited tensely in her bedroom until she saw the light come on under the communicating door, then made herself go and knock.

It had opened instantly to reveal Renzo, his shirt already half-unbuttoned and his expression wary.

'*Sì?*' His brusque tone did not encourage her either,

nor the fact that he didn't seem to notice she was once again wearing only a nightgown.

Marisa held out a folded piece of paper. She said stiltedly, 'I—I wrote down that—information that you wanted.'

He took it from her, his face expressionless as he scanned the brief list of dates she'd provided.

Then, *'Grazie tante,'* he drawled, slipping it into his pants pocket. 'You are all consideration, *mia cara*, and I shall try to follow your example. But to my sorrow, I shall not be able to keep our first appointment. I have to go to Boston on business.' He paused, his wintry smile not reaching his eyes. 'Unless, of course, you wish to accompany me, *mia sposa*, in order that the opportunity is not wasted?'

'I hardly think so.' She looked down at the floor, aware that this was not going as she'd dared to hope. 'Emilio is still showing me the house—explaining my new responsibilities, how everything works. Besides, I really do need to buy some clothes before I go on any trips, and Ottavia has offered to take me shopping in Firenze.'

'Then I shall count the hours until the next occasion,' Renzo said too gently. 'I must tell my secretary to mark it in my diary.'

'Don't,' she whispered, still not looking at him. 'Please—don't.'

'I think perhaps that should be my line, not yours,' he said, and shrugged. *'Tuttavia—non importa. Buona notte*, Maria Lisa. Sleep well.'

He'd stepped back, and the door had closed between them.

But it wasn't just the door, Marisa thought now, sighing as she picked up the book she was struggling to read. All other lines of communication had been shut off too. No phone calls this time. And no letters either.

I miss him, she told herself, the breath catching in her throat. *I miss him so terribly.*

After all, it was in this house that she'd first started to fall in love with him, even when she had been too young to know what love meant.

But she knew now—knew it in all its aspects. And while she could stay busy by day, learning to be the mistress of the Villa Proserpina, her nights, whether she was awake or dreaming, were a continuing torment, her body on fire for an appeasement that never came.

Her imagination tortured with the thought that by now he would have taken her at her word and be sharing his bed with another woman.

Restlessly, she rose and walked across to the long windows, pushing them open and stepping out on to the *loggia.* The earlier rain had stopped, leaving the air filled with the scent of wet blossoms, and she stood, leaning on the balustrade, as she drew the fragrance deeply into her lungs.

I could be so happy here, she thought. *Whereas the most I can hope for is—acceptance.*

And she paused, tensing, as she heard in the distance the sound of a car approaching down the avenue.

Oh, God, she thought, her throat tightening in mingled fear and longing. Renzo—it must be Renzo. No one else was due.

She glanced down at her black cotton trousers and their matching shirt, her hand going to the clip confining her scraped-back hair at the nape of her neck. She was not going to meet him like this—not when she had cupboards full of new clothes, thanks to the good offices of Ottavia Arlesconi.

She was pulling off her things as she ran to the bedroom. Seconds later she was in the shower, emerging breathlessly after a couple of minutes to dry herself and apply scented lotion to her skin, spraying the matching perfume on her throat, her breasts and thighs.

She scrambled into her newest and prettiest white lace underwear and put on a straight linen dress, beautifully cut, in a soft misty green, sliding her feet into low-heeled pumps.

She brushed her hair until it crackled, then applied a coating of mascara to her lashes and some soft colour to her mouth.

It occurred to her that she'd not heard Renzo come up to the suite, or go into his room. No doubt he had stayed to talk to his father.

She wanted to run, but she made herself walk calmly and sedately downstairs. There would be time later to demonstrate how eager she was to see him again, she thought, her pulses hammering.

As she reached the entrance hall, Emilio was coming towards the stairs, carrying a travel bag and a briefcase.

She took a breath. Tried to sound casual. 'I thought I heard a car, Emilio. Has someone arrived?'

'*Sì, signora.*' He beamed, indicating the door of the *salotto*.

Try and play it cool, Marisa adjured herself as she pushed open the door. *But make sure you let him see that you're—pleased.*

She walked forward and halted, her throat closing with shock and disappointment. For the room's only occupant was Ottavia Arlesconi, seated on a sofa and glancing through a fashion magazine.

She glanced up with her usual calm friendliness. '*Ciao*, Marisa. *Come sta?*'

'Ottavia—how lovely.' She forced herself to smile. 'I didn't know you'd be here this weekend.'

'A last-minute decision.' The other woman spread her hands. 'Guillermo called me, and I could not refuse.' She studied Marisa with a faint frown. 'Are you quite well? You look a little pale.'

'I'm fine.' She took a seat, smoothing her skirt with nervous hands. 'I—I thought it might be Renzo's car.'

The *signora* put down her magazine. 'Renzo—here?' She shook her head. 'I don't think he is expected.' She paused. 'But you have received a different message, perhaps?'

There was a silence, then Marisa said quietly, 'No. No message.'

'Ah,' said the *signora*. There was another, longer silence, then Ottavia said, 'Marisa, you have no mother. I—I have no daughter, and maybe I am not qualified to speak, but I cannot stay silent when I see how unhappy you are.' She hesitated. 'It is no secret that your marriage has been troubled from the first. But when you returned here with Lorenzo we all hoped that you might find a life together.'

'Not quite all.' Marisa's hands gripped together in her lap.

'The woman is a witch,' Ottavia said calmly. 'We need not regard her. My concern is the words you spoke to her, and which Lorenzo heard. I saw him at breakfast the next morning and he looked grey—like a ghost. And when he left the following day he was alone.' She looked steadily at Marisa. 'As he has been, I think, since your marriage.'

She paused. 'I do not count the foolishness with the Venucci woman,' she went on, and held up a placatory hand as Marisa stiffened. 'Nor do I condone it, believe me. But when a man is hurt and lonely he will sometimes find comfort in the wrong place. And you were hardly around to object,' she added dryly.

Marisa bent her head. 'No,' she said with constraint. 'I stayed away because it's never been a real marriage. Renzo never wanted a wife—and he wanted me least of all.'

'Perhaps he was reluctant at first,' Ottavia said slowly. 'But after you became engaged that changed.

He was quiet, thoughtful, when he returned from London, making plans for the wedding and where you would live. He wished everything to be perfect for you. He was also nervous, which I had never seen before.' She smiled suddenly. 'It made me like him better. And also think that he wished to be married to you very much.'

'Because he needed someone to give him a son and not make demands on his time and attention that he could not fulfil,' Marisa said tonelessly. 'I—fitted the template.'

'Is that why you are so determined not to love him?' Ottavia asked gently. 'Why you demonstrate to the world that he means nothing to you by leaving him for months on end? Why you even proclaim it aloud in front of him—treating him without kindness or respect?'

She shook her head. '*Dio mio*, is it any wonder that he stays away?'

Marisa said with difficulty, 'There might be another reason. Something I practically pushed him into.' She paused. 'Ottavia—has he got another woman?'

'I do not know,' the older woman returned. 'And if I knew, my dear child, I would not tell you. But I will say this,' she added more robustly. 'If I was a girl in love with a man as attractive as Lorenzo, I would not make the mistake of turning him out of my bed a second time. I would make sure I was always the one at his side when he slept.'

'Because you'd know you couldn't trust him?' It hurt to say it.

'No,' Ottavia said with emphasis. 'Because I could not bear to be apart from him. But if you cannot forgive his past errors with your whole heart, there is no more to be said.'

Marisa said in a low voice, 'Suppose he doesn't want to be forgiven? That he's had enough?'

Ottavia shrugged. 'That, *cara*, is a risk you will have to take. But in your shoes I would fight—and fight again.'

I already did that, Marisa thought as she left the room. *But it turned out to be the wrong battle. And now, heaven help me, I may never get another chance.*

CHAPTER TWELVE

SHE could, she supposed, follow Renzo to Rome, Marisa thought as she trailed slowly upstairs, her mind whirling. Try and talk to him.

But what on earth was she going to say? And anyway, after everything that had happened between them would he even be prepared to listen?

And suppose he wasn't alone...

Fight, Ottavia had said. But if it came down to that what kind of fight would it be? A stand-up, knock-down, hair-pulling, eye-scratching brawl with some glamorous Roman beauty, and Renzo as referee? That was a hideous prospect, she thought, shuddering inwardly. Besides, there was no guarantee she'd win.

She walked back into the *salotto* and closed the door. Late-afternoon sun was pouring in, filling the room with real warmth. Maybe it was a good omen, she thought. Or perhaps she was going a little crazy in the head, looking for signs and portents in the weather. Because at this time of the year storms were never far away.

She put on some more music—not Puccini, this

time; not more love lost, love betrayed—but some lilting guitar and harp concertos.

Curling back into the corner of her sofa, she looked down at her hands, twisting her wedding ring on her finger. Something Ottavia had said was forcing itself back into her mind. 'When a man is hurt and lonely...'

Hurt, she thought, trying the words for herself, as if she was learning a foreign language. *Lonely?*

Hardly a description to apply to Lorenzo the Magnificent, who stalked through life, taking from it exactly what he wanted, making his own rules and expecting to be obeyed with one crook of his little finger.

And the last man in the world that she should ever have fallen in love with, she acknowledged with a swift, unhappy sigh. Or tried to live without...

She leaned back against the cushions, closing her eyes, letting the music soothe her, and the gentle golden heat permeate to the marrow of her bones, feeling relaxed for the first time in a long while.

Maybe she should spend her nights here on the sofa, she thought wryly, rather than in that big bed with all its memories. All its bitter regrets.

Perhaps, too, she would sleep without dreams she didn't want to remember in the morning. Or even no dreams at all.

And yet, as the weariness engendered by so many restless nights finally overcame her and she slept, she dreamed she was sinking down into a field of golden flowers, stretching around her as far as the eye could see. And as she turned her head, trying to capture a breath of their faint, elusive scent, she felt the blossoms brush her hair and the curve of her cheek.

The next instant the field had gone, transformed into an ordinary sofa again, and she was sitting up, eyes wide open and her heart pounding, wondering what had woken her.

She heard, not too far away, the soft sound of a closing door.

Rosalia, she thought. Coming as usual to ask what the *signora* wished to wear for dinner. Except it was much too early for that, as one startled glance at her watch confirmed.

It might have been Ottavia, of course, checking that their conversation earlier had not upset her. But the older woman would never visit this part of the house without an invitation, and neither would Guillermo, she was sure. They would both regard it as an invasion of privacy, whether Renzo was there or not.

Renzo…

With sudden shock, she remembered the subtle fragrance she'd encountered in her dream, and knew why it had seemed so strangely familiar—and so enticing.

It was his cologne, she thought, the one he always used, understated and expensive. As much a part of him as the colour of his eyes and the texture of his skin.

And it could only mean that he was here—somewhere. And that, however briefly, he'd been close to her. Maybe—touched her.

But it also meant that he'd found her asleep, slumped inelegantly, and, in a worst-case ever scenario, possibly even snoring—with her mouth open.

'Oh, God,' she muttered as she scrambled off the sofa, pushing back her dishevelled hair from her face, trying to straighten her creased dress, searching for and then abandoning her kicked-off shoes. 'Not that—please.'

She flew barefoot along the passage to her bedroom, but it was empty. She halted, a hand going to her mouth like a disappointed child.

Only to realise that the communicating door was standing half-open for the first time in weeks, and someone was moving around in the adjoining room.

Marisa walked across and pushed the door wide.

Renzo was there, crossing with an armful of shirts to the leather suitcase lying open on the bed.

She said his name quietly, almost tentatively, and he turned immediately, his brows lifting.

'Marisa.' He might be casually dressed, in blue pants and a matching half-buttoned shirt, but that was where the informality ended, because his tone was polite to the point of bleakness. 'I disturbed you. *La prego di accettare le mie scuse.*'

'There's no need to apologise,' she said quickly. 'I was just dozing in the sunshine.' She swallowed. 'I thought—I understood you wouldn't be here today.'

'I did not intend to be.' He began to put the shirts into the case. 'But I find I now have to go to Stockholm, then on to Brussels, and I need some extra things for the trip.' He paused. 'But you need not worry,' he added coolly. 'As soon as my packing is done I shall be returning to Rome.'

'You mean—tonight?'

'I mean in the next half-hour.' His tone was brusque.

'But you haven't been home—to stay—for quite some time.' *Which I could itemise in days, hours, and minutes.*

'And that is a problem?' His mouth twisted. 'I thought it would be a relief.'

'But not for your father, certainly. He—must miss you very much.'

'If so, it is strange that he did not mention it when I spoke to him on the telephone this morning. As I do each day.'

But you've never asked to talk to me, she thought, pain slashing at her anew. *Or even sent me a message...*

She said slowly, 'I—didn't know that.'

'*Certo che no.* Obviously not. However, there is no need for you to concern yourself on his behalf. He understands the situation.'

'Then perhaps you'd explain it to me.' Marisa lifted her chin. 'I thought I would see you—at least sometimes.'

'Ah,' he said softly. 'On the occasions you were good enough to list for me, no doubt?' He shrugged. 'Unfortunately I have quite enough meetings and agendas in my working day, *mia cara*. I find, therefore, I have no wish for them to invade my private life.' And he resumed his task.

Marisa could feel her throat tightening. Was aware that she was beginning to tremble inside once more.

She said, 'And if I—asked you to stay?'

He turned slowly, his face expressionless.

He said quietly, 'Give me one good reason why I should do so.'

She looked back at him—at the hooded watchful eyes and the firm mouth that seemed as if they would never smile again. At the lean body that had taught her with gentleness and skill such an infinity of pleasure. And she could sense tension flowing like an electrical current between them.

Hurt, she thought. *Lonely...*

And her mind became suddenly and quite magically clear.

She said, softly and simply, 'Because I want you.'

She waited for him to come to her—to take her in his arms—but he stayed where he was, putting the last shirt almost too carefully into place.

And when he spoke his voice was harsh. 'Prove it.'

For a moment she stood, frozen, as she realised what he was asking. As all her insecurities threatened to come flooding back to defeat her.

She thought, *I can't...*

Only to recognise, once again, that she had no choice. That this could be her last chance, and she had to make it work—had to...

And if this is all he'll ever require from me, she thought, *then—so be it.*

Without haste, she began to release the first of the buttons that fastened the green dress from neckline to hem, holding his eyes with hers.

When she'd undone them all, she shrugged the dress from her shoulders, unhooked her bra and let it drop, cupping her breasts with her fingers, watching the flare of colour along his cheekbones. She allowed her hands to drift down to the edge of her lace briefs, and pause teasingly as she smiled at him, touching her parted lips with the tip of her tongue.

As she uncovered herself completely for the intensity of his gaze.

She moved slowly across the space that divided them until she was within touching distance, then, remembering what she'd believed was a dream, she put up a hand to stroke his hair, before running her fingers, delicate as the petals of a flower, down the strong line of his face to the faint roughness of his chin.

Her hands slid down, freeing the remaining buttons on his shirt, pushing its edges wide apart so that her fingers had the liberty to roam over his shoulders and bare chest. To feel the clench of his muscles and experience the sudden unsteadiness of his heartbeat as she deliberately tantalised the flat male nipples, feeling them harden as she moved closer to brush them with the aroused peaks of her own breasts.

She began to touch him with her lips, planting tiny fugitive kisses all over the warm skin as her hands slid down to deal with the waistband of his trousers, pausing, the breath catching in her throat, as her fingers flickered on the iron-hardness beneath the fabric and heard his soft groan of response.

She tugged at his zip, then dragged the heavy fabric over his hips and down to the floor, so that he could step free of it. Then her fingers returned to release his powerfully aroused shaft from the cling of his silk shorts and, shyly at first, to caress him.

She felt his hand move in its turn, tangling in the soft fall of her hair, holding her still as his mouth came down on hers, his kiss hard and deep, his tongue probing all her inner sweetness.

Then, still kissing her, he lifted her into his arms and carried her into the other room and across to their bed.

There was no gentle wooing this time. No slow ascent to pleasure. Their mutual hunger was too strong, too urgent for that. Instead, he stripped off his shorts and sank into her, filling her, as he gasped his need against her parted lips. And Marisa arched against him, her body surging in a reply as rapturous as it was uncontrollable.

Almost before they knew it they had reached the agonised extremity of desire. Marisa sobbed into his mouth as she felt the first quivers of sensual delight ripple through her innermost being, then deepen voluptuously until her entire body was shaken, torn apart by a series of harsh, exquisite convulsions bordering on savagery. She called his name, half in fear, half in exultation, as the sensations reached their peak, and heard in the next instant his hoarse cry of pleasure as his body found its own scalding, shuddering release in hers.

Afterwards they lay wrapped together, exchanging slow, sweet kisses.

'Was that proof enough?' Marisa asked at last, nibbling softly at his lower lip.

'Let us say a beginning, perhaps. No more,' Renzo returned lazily, his fingers curving round her breast. 'You may, however, become more convincing in Stockholm,' he added musingly. 'And by the time we reach Brussels I may even start to believe that I have a wife.'

Her eyes widened. 'You're taking me with you?'

'I have no intention of leaving you behind, *carissima*. Not again. Rosalia can pack for you while we're having dinner.'

'But I thought you wanted to leave straight away.'

'I have changed my mind,' he said. 'I expect to be far too exhausted to drive anywhere tonight.' He moved deliberately. Significantly. 'With your co-operation, of course, *signora*.'

'I'll try to be of assistance, *signore*,' Marisa whispered, and lifted her smiling mouth to his.

But later, when he'd fallen into a light sleep, and she lay in his arms, her head pillowed on his shoulder,

Marisa found the echoing tremors of delight were being replaced by an odd sadness.

Wife, she thought. At last she was his wife. But for how long would he want her? Until she'd justified her presence in his life—when he would have no further cause to play the passionate husband?

That was the uneasy possibility that was now suggesting itself.

Because her insistence on leading an independent life once she'd given him an heir might well turn out to be a two-edged sword.

The purpose of their marriage achieved, Renzo, too, would be free to live as he wished—even to renew the bachelor existence that had caused so much trouble between them in the past.

She knew herself better now, she thought wryly, so she could recognise that it was not dislike or indifference which had created the rift at the start of their marriage, but plain old-fashioned jealousy.

Julia's reference to Lucia Gallo had quietly gnawed away at her throughout her engagement, freezing her emotions and convincing her she would rather do without him altogether than share his attentions with another girl.

Her heart told her that she would feel no differently if there was a similar situation in the future. Indeed, it would be worse now that she had learned the meaning of delight in his arms.

And she thought painfully, there would be

nothing she could do about it next time but accept—and suffer.

And remember that once, for a little while, he'd belonged to her completely.

'My dear Signora Santangeli,' Dr Fabiano said gently. 'I am sure that you are allowing yourself to worry without necessity over this matter.' He put down his pen and smiled at her. He was a tall, rather stooped man with a goatee beard and kind eyes behind rimless glasses. 'You have only been married for just over a year, I think.'

'Yes,' Marisa admitted. 'But I thought—by now—it might have happened.'

Especially, she thought, as she and Renzo had spent the past three months in the passionate and uninhibited enjoyment of each other's bodies, without any precautions whatsoever.

He'd said nothing more about learning to be man and wife. The imperative now was the continuation of the Santangeli name.

'And we both want a child so much,' she added.

Renzo needs his heir, she thought, *and I—I just wish him to have his heart's desire. To please him in this special way because I love him so desperately. And because if I give him the son he wants then I might begin to mean more to him than just the girl currently in his bed.*

He—he might start to—love me in return. Because he's never said that he does, or even hinted it.

Not before. Not when we've been going half-crazy in each other's arms. And not afterwards when he holds me as we sleep. When perhaps I need to hear it most.

'Sometimes nature likes to take its own time,' the doctor said easily. 'Also, *signora*, your husband may not wish to share you just yet.' He paused. 'Or does he share your anxieties?'

'We haven't really discussed it,' Marisa said. In fact, if she was completely honest, she admitted silently, the subject hadn't been mentioned at all. Or not out loud, anyway.

However physically attuned she and Renzo might have become, there were still no-go areas in the marriage. Subjects they walked around rather than introduced as topics into the conversation.

But she was aware that Renzo watched her quite often, as if he was—waiting for something.

She took a breath, 'I expect it's all my imagination, *dottore*, but as the weeks pass I do find myself wondering if everything's all right. With me, that is.'

He looked surprised. 'I have your notes from your doctor in England. Your general health seems excellent, and at the moment, Signora Santangeli, I would say you were glowing.'

'I feel fine,' she said, flushing a little. 'I suppose I'm just looking for—reassurance.'

'Because this would be a precious child.' He smiled at her. 'Perhaps a future Marchese Santangeli. I understand, of course.'

He paused thoughtfully. 'There are, of course, tests we can do—examinations that can be carried out. Usually I would not recommend them after so short a marriage—but if they put your mind at rest they could be useful. What do you think?'

She said, 'I think they could be exactly what I need.'

'Then I will make the necessary arrangements.' He pulled a pad towards him and began to scribble something on it. 'You will naturally tell your husband what you are planning?'

'Of course,' she said.

When it's all over and done with, and I know that it's just a question of patience and perseverance, because everything's fine. I'll tell him then, and we'll laugh about it.

Marisa was thoughtful as she drove home later. Uneasy too.

But she had to believe she'd just made a positive move. One that could change her life for the better.

As if it hadn't already altered in innumerable ways, she thought wryly. The fact that she had a driving licence and a car of her own now was only one of them. Yet she couldn't help remembering Renzo's quiet words as he had put the keys in her hand. 'A step towards your freedom, *mia cara.*'

Had he been reminding her that, despite the passion they shared, their present intimacy was only transient, and that one day their paths would permanently diverge?

No, she told herself, keep being positive. Apart from anything else, she was now the accepted mistress of the Villa Proserpina. If the staff had looked at her askance in the days of her estrangement from Renzo, she now basked in their approval.

And she had Zio Guillermo's whole-hearted support too. She could still see the expression of joyful incredulity on his face when she'd entered the *salotto* that first evening, shy but radiant, with Renzo's arm around her and his hand resting on her hip in a gesture of unmistakable possession.

And she had heard his muttered, 'At last—may the good God be praised.'

Later, when they could not be overheard, Ottavia too had whispered teasingly, 'I see the fight is over, *cara*, but I will not ask who won.'

And she'd started to travel too. Whenever possible Renzo insisted on taking her with him on his business trips, and gradually, with his encouragement, she'd begun to feel less gauche on the inevitable social occasions, was able to hold her own at cocktail parties and formal dinners, even once overhearing herself described as 'charming'.

When she'd repeated this to Renzo later, he'd merely grinned wickedly and drawled, 'I am glad that they cannot know precisely how charming you are at this moment, *mia bella*,' letting his mouth drift slowly and sensuously down her naked body.

The apartment in Rome was no longer unknown territory for her either. But her initial visit had almost sparked off a quarrel between them. Because that first night there, when he'd taken her in his arms, she'd found it difficult to relax, her imagination going haywire as she wondered, despite herself, who else had shared this particular bed with him.

'Is something wrong?' His hand had captured her chin, making her look at him.

'It's nothing,' she'd said, too quickly. 'Really—I'm fine.'

His mouth had tightened. 'Then remain so by avoiding unwise speculation,' he'd advised coldly. 'Because no other woman has ever stayed here. Not on moral grounds,' he'd added cynically. 'But because in the past I have always valued my privacy too highly. Perhaps I was wise.' And he'd turned over and gone to sleep.

He'd woken her around dawn, offering reconciliation with the ardour of his lovemaking, and it had never been mentioned again.

But Marisa had seen it as a warning that references to his past were now strictly taboo. And presumably the same sanction would apply to any future *amours* he might engage in.

He would be discreet, and would expect her, in turn, to be blind. Probably dumb too, she thought, and sighed.

But whatever happened she would still be his wife, with all the courtesies her status demanded. She would wear his ring, and manage his homes and raise their children.

Those were her rights, she told herself. No one could take them away from her.

And in spite of the heat of the day, she felt herself shivering.

'You are going where?' Ottavia asked, her brows lifting in astonishment.

'To the Clinica San Francesco,' Marisa said, her throat tightening. 'Just for a day—overnight, perhaps. Apparently Dr Fabiano wants me to have another more detailed examination.'

She looked down at her hands. 'And as I may not feel like driving immediately afterwards, I wondered if you'd be good enough to take me there in your car—and bring me back.'

'But this should be for Lorenzo to do,' the *signora* protested. 'He should not be in Zurich, but here with you. I am astonished that he should absent himself at such a time.'

Marisa was silent for a moment, then she said reluctantly, 'Renzo doesn't know.'

Ottavia's jaw dropped. 'You have not told him?'

Marisa shook her head. 'Not about the initial tests,

or this—new development.' She paused. 'I cried off from Zurich—told him I had a tummy upset because I didn't want to worry him.'

'I think you should worry for yourself,' Ottavia told her grimly. 'When he finds out he will be very angry.' She groaned. 'Guillermo too, I think.' She took Marisa's hands in hers. 'Be advised, *cara*. You know where Renzo can be contacted. Ask him to come home and tell him everything.'

'But there may not be anything to tell,' Marisa said. 'In which case I'll have brought him back from an important round of meetings for no reason.' She tried to smile. 'He might not be very pleased about that either.'

'Another risk you should take.'

'I'd much rather deal with it by myself. There are so many problems in the financial markets these days that I don't want to burden him with anything else. Especially if it turns out to be some kind of—glitch.'

She looked appealingly at the other woman. 'So, will you do this for me? I—I have no one else I can ask.'

Ottavia sighed. 'When you put it like that—yes.' She hesitated. 'But understand this, Marisa, I will not lie for you on this matter. If Renzo returns and asks where you are, or Guillermo comes back early from Milano with the same question, then I shall tell them. *Capisce?*'

'Yes,' Marisa said steadily. 'I do understand. But I'm sure it won't be necessary, and I shall be back here long before either of them.' She took a deep breath. 'No harm done.'

She was praying wordlessly, as she'd done every day since the first tests, that it would be no more than the truth.

CHAPTER THIRTEEN

SHE couldn't stop crying. Ever since she'd looked at the grave, concerned faces at the foot of her bed, and realised that her inexplicable uneasiness was fully justified after all, tears had never been far away.

And now they were there, possessing, destroying her. Eyes blinded, throat raw with the long choking sobs, she could not... stop.

Although she'd been icily, deadly calm when they'd told her what she'd insisted on knowing, dismissing their protests that she should not be alone—that her husband, that Signor Lorenzo must be sent for while she heard what the tests and examinations had actually revealed.

When they had admitted with the utmost reluctance that there was something—not a simple matter of infertility alone, which could be treated, but a malformation of some kind—which, in the unlikely event that she ever conceived, would not allow her to carry the child full-term.

She'd said, in a voice she had not recognised, 'But there must be something to rectify the condition.'

She'd bitten her lip until she tasted blood. 'Surely some kind of operation…?'

And had listened to the gentle, lengthy explanations, full of medical terms that she did not fully comprehend. But then she didn't have to. Because she understood only too well that beneath the compassion and the technicalities they were telling her no. There was nothing. Nothing…

As somehow she had already known, with some strange, inexplicable female instinct. She'd felt that strange fear like a black shadow in the corner of her life, getting closer with every day that passed, until it blotted out the sun and left her in the cold dark.

But at least now, she could be alone with her misery—her aching, uncontrollable despair.

The nursing staff, so hideously well-meaning as they fluttered around her with offers of water to drink, to wash her face, to help swallow a sedative, had finally been persuaded to leave. And they'd clearly been glad to go, hardly knowing what to do for this patient—this girl—this wife, *Santa Madonna*, of such an important man. So powerful, so attractive, so virile. Yet doomed, it seemed, through no one's fault, to be the last of his ancient name.

Small wonder that she felt such grief, they agreed as they left, glancing back at the slim, hunched shape in the bed. For who would wish to disappoint such a husband?

He had been sent for, of course. The Director had

intervened personally, horrified that such information should have been given to Signor Santangeli's young wife in his absence. And now he was on his way.

But in the meantime the *signora* needed comfort, and who better than an older woman, a member of the family—her husband's own grandmother, no less—who was at the Clinica, the Director had learned, visiting a friend.

Which was why Marisa, having wept herself hollow, looked up from her soaking pillow as her door opened and saw Teresa Barzati advancing into the room.

She said in a small, cracked voice, 'What are you doing here?'

'I came to visit the Contessa Morico, who is recovering from a hip replacement. And now I find I have another errand of mercy.' The *signora* deposited herself in the room's solitary armchair, her thin lips stretched in an unpleasant smile. 'To bring you the consolation of a grandmother. Or should I keep that for Lorenzo, when he arrives from Zurich?'

Marisa made herself sit up and push the damp strands of hair back from her white face. Made herself look stonily back at the last person in the world she wanted to see. 'I don't think Renzo will wish to see you any more than I do,' she said. 'After the trouble you tried to make for us.'

The *signora*'s smile widened. 'I doubt you have the right to speak for my grandson,' she said. 'Not any longer. And the trouble you find yourself in at this moment has quite eclipsed anything I could do. Because you have failed, *signora*. According to the rumours all over the hospital you are incapable of bearing children.' She paused. 'Or, by some miracle, are these whispers wrong?'

Marisa thought with an odd detachment, as the older woman's eyes bored remorselessly into her, that it was like being mesmerised by a cobra. That even though you knew the death blow would be delivered at any moment you still could not look away. Or move to safety.

The stranger's voice she'd heard earlier said, 'No, they're—not wrong.'

Nonna Teresa nodded with a kind of terrible satisfaction. 'And what a heavy blow that will be for the Santangeli pride.' She paused. 'For a while, anyway. Until they acknowledge the mistake they have made with you and move on.'

She sighed. 'Poor Guillermo. I almost pity him. This alliance—planned for so long, arranged with such care—totally in ruins. The delicate path that he and Lorenzo must now tread, so that they do not appear too heartless when they bring the marriage to its end.'

'What are you talking about?'

'About you, Marisa. What else? About how Lorenzo will set you aside so that he can marry again. And next time, if he has sense,' she added cuttingly, 'he will choose some strong, fertile Italian bride who will do his bidding and know her place.'

'That won't happen.' She'd thought that she was

quite empty, devoid of all emotion. But she had not allowed for the power of a different kind of pain. The kind that cut so deeply that you felt you might bleed to death, slowly and endlessly. She rallied herself. 'Lorenzo doesn't believe in divorce. He's always said so.'

'Divorce, no. That would indeed be too shocking,' Nonna Teresa said smoothly. 'But there are always grounds for annulment to be found, if you have influence in the right places. And Lorenzo and his father are supremely influential.' Her laugh was melodious. 'A barren wife will prove small obstacle to their plans for the future, believe me.'

Marisa stared at her in a kind of awful fascination. She said, 'How can you do this, *signora*? How can you come here at a time like this and say these things to me.'

'Because I almost feel sorry for you,' Signora Barzati returned. 'You were bought for a purpose, as you admitted yourself. And like most items that are damaged or otherwise unsuitable, you are about to be returned. But your departure will be cushioned,' she added negligently. 'You will not be dismissed as a pauper. Guillermo will make sure of that. In spite of this unsuitable liaison with the Alesconi woman, he still has sufficient respect for my late daughter's memory to adhere to her wishes in that regard.'

'I don't believe one word of this.' Marisa's voice was shaking. She reached up to the bell beside her bed. 'I won't believe it. Now I'd like you to get out.'

The *signora* stayed where she was. 'But I am trying to be your friend, Marisa. To explain frankly what lies ahead for you. I thought you would be grateful.'

'Grateful to be told that I'm going to be thrown aside by my husband like a piece of junk?' Marisa asked hoarsely.

'Hardly,' Nonna Teresa said reprovingly. 'That is not the Santangeli way. I am certain he will be kind to you. As long as you understand you no longer have any part in his life and accept your departure with grace.'

She played with the ring on her hand.

Another emerald, Marisa thought, her eyes drawn against her will to the green flash of the stone. And for the rest of my life I shall always hate emeralds.

'Besides, this should be good news for you,' the *Signora* went on musingly. 'You never wished to be Lorenzo's wife, and made your indifference to him quite clear. In front of him, too, as I recall. Now you will be single again, and he can find another wife, more to his taste.' She smiled, her glance raking the tearstained face and slender body. 'It should not be difficult. And then everyone will have what they want, is that not so?'

The questioning silence seemed endless. Then she said softly, 'Or perhaps not. Is it possible, my dear Marisa, that you have had a change of heart? Can you have mistaken my grandson's performance of his marital duties for something warmer and been foolish enough to fall in love with him?'

She laughed again, contemptuously. 'I do believe it is so. What a truly pathetic child you are if you imagine you have ever been more to Lorenzo than a willing body in his bed. One of so many.' She examined a nail. 'And although he may have been assiduous in his attentions while he thought you might provide the Santangeli heir, now that he knows the truth he will no longer have to pretend. And how will you like that?'

Marisa felt naked under the scorn in those inimical eyes. The fact that her heart was breaking was not enough for this monstrous woman, she thought, fighting sudden nausea. Every last shred of pride and dignity had to be stripped from her too.

She said slowly, 'You've always hated me. And you didn't like my mother. I can remember things you said when I was small, and Zia Maria being upset about them.'

'You are quite right,' the older woman agreed. 'I detested your mother, and wished my daughter had never met her. My husband was a fool, and worse than a fool to insist that she should go to a school where she could make such friends—betray me and all I held dear. I never forgave him for it. However, I made sure that my child, my beloved Maria, married well—only to find she intended to contaminate the Santangeli blood with that of an outsider, an enemy.' She brought a clenched fist down on the arm of her chair. '*Dio mio*—that she could do such a thing.'

'But I never wished to be your enemy, *signora*.' Marisa was shaken by the older woman's furious vehemence. 'And nor did my parents.'

'You? You think I ever cared about you? It was what you were—you and all your family.' Signora Barzati's voice rose. 'You were British—part of the cursed nation that caused my most beloved brother, noble in every way, to die as a prisoner of war in North Africa and to be buried in some unmarked grave in the desert. To know that you were destined for my grandson was an insult to his glorious memory.'

Oh, God, Marisa thought, dry-mouthed. *This is crazy. The war's been over for more than sixty years. Teresa was little more than a child when it happened. And yet to carry such a grudge—to hate all this time. It beggars belief. But it explains so much, too.*

She said quietly, 'But there has been peace for a long time, *signora*. And forgiveness.'

'Virtues you admire, perhaps?' Signora Barzati had herself under control again, leaning back in her chair. 'And soon you will have a chance to practise them, if you choose. Will you do so, Marisa? Will you let Lorenzo think that you spoke nothing but the truth when you said you did not love him and did not care about your marriage? Will you sign the annulment papers and leave peacefully, taking your sad little secret with you?

'And when you are living alone in England, without even the illusion of Lorenzo's love to comfort you,

will you forgive him for not caring for you in return—
and for letting you go so easily? You could do all that
and earn some goodwill on your departure, if you
wished. Even a little respect.'

She paused. 'Or you could make more trouble by
attempting to remain where you are not wanted—and
of no further use. By embarrassing Lorenzo with your
protestations of devotion. Nothing will prevent you
being sent away. But you have a choice in the way it
is done.' She smiled. 'In your shoes I would go of my
own accord. I would jump, as they say, before I was
pushed. But the decision, *naturalamente*, is yours.'

She rose, smoothing the skirt of her dark dress. 'I
say this for your own good, you understand. There is
no sense in making a bad situation worse, and I am
sure you see that. That you are not such a fool as
to…hope. Because the Santangeli family will do as
it must, and you can either survive—or be crushed.'

She walked to the door, then turned, her voice throbbing with sudden emotion. 'And if you think I have been
cruel, imagine how you would feel, holding out your
arms to the man you desire more than all the world and
watching him turn away. Knowing that he will never
want you again. If you still do not believe me, try it when
Lorenzo comes here. Reach for him—if you dare.'

And she was gone.

By the time she heard the faint hubbub in the corridor
signalling that Renzo had arrived, Marisa had

prepared herself. Made sure she was under control. That she would not weep. Would not beg.

And that she would not take the risk of reaching for him and being rejected. That most of all.

After the *signora* had left she had lain, staring into space, with eyes that burned and saw nothing.

With a mind that had heard only the ugly, corrosive words that had told her what she'd already known in her heart. That the doctors' verdict had not simply passed sentence on her hope of a baby, but also on her marriage.

That Teresa Barzati, however uncaring and malign, had spoken only the truth. If she could not fulfil the purpose for which she'd been married she would have to step aside. She would have no choice.

Therefore she must try not to think of these last rapturous months with Renzo. Must remember only that he would have seen them ultimately as a means to an end. That an eager and co-operative wife was much to be preferred to a girl who received his advances with sullen resentment.

But that sexual passion, however skilful and generous, did not equate with the kind of love that could weather all the storms that life sent.

It would be so much easier for me now, she thought with dull weariness, *if I'd let myself go on thinking that I hated him. That I didn't want any part of marriage to him.*

If I hadn't let myself love him, and hope that one day he would tell me that he loved me in return.

Yet he never did. Even in our most intimate moments he never said the words I longed to hear. And now he never will. And that, somehow, will be the worst thing I have to bear.

Because I need his arms round me. Need to feel the shelter of his warmth and strength.

But it wasn't only the loss of his lovemaking—those moments when he lifted her up to touch the stars—that she would mourn. There were all the small things—her hand in his when they walked together, the private smiles across a table or a room. The conversations about everything and nothing as they shared the sofa in the *salotto*, or lay wrapped in each other's arms, all passion spent.

Learning, she'd thought, to be husband and wife, just as he'd once suggested. Forging a bond that could never be broken.

And now, because of nature's cruellest trick, her dreams of the future lay in pieces.

And somehow she had to find the strength to walk away and build a different kind of life. Without him.

A withdrawal that would have to begin as soon as he came through that door.

She had done what she could to look calm and in control, even if her emotions were like shards of broken glass. She'd washed her face, and put drops in her eyes to conceal the worst ravages. She'd changed into a fresh nightgown and brushed her hair. Even added a touch of lipstick to her pale mouth.

He came slowly into the room, closed the door and leaned against it, staring at her, his eyes shadowed, his mouth a bleak line.

Marisa realised she'd been holding her breath, praying silently that he would come across the room and take her in his arms. That he would somehow do the unthinkable—the impossible—and make it all right.

But her prayer was not answered, and instead she heard herself say quietly, 'Have the doctors told you?'

'Yes,' he said. 'I now know everything.'

She looked down at the edge of the crisp white sheet. 'I—I'm so sorry.'

'And I am sorry too,' he said. 'That you did not tell me of your concerns. That you chose instead to bear this alone, so that I had to be...summoned to hear these things. Why did you do this?'

'Because I didn't want to worry you,' she said. 'Not if it was all in my imagination, as Dr Fabiano originally thought.'

'But later,' he said. 'When it became more than a suspicion. You still let me walk away—leave for Zurich without you.'

'It might still have been just a glitch.' She could hear the pleading note in her voice and suppressed it. 'Something easily put right. And life goes on.'

But not life inside me—life that you put there...

'Yes,' he said. 'Life goes on.' He was very still for a moment, then he sighed, and straightened. 'I have been told that I must not stay too long. That more than anything you need rest. Accordingly, the consultant has recommended that you remain here for another day. So I will come for you tomorrow, after I have spoken with my father, and then we must talk, you and I.'

'Couldn't you do that now?' she said. 'Say what you have to say?'

'It is too soon,' he said. 'I have to clear my mind— to think. But tomorrow it will be different. And then we will speak.'

'Until tomorrow, then.' With a superhuman effort she managed to say the words without her voice cracking in the middle.

He looked at her, and for a moment she saw the faint ghost of his old smile. 'Until then,' he said. 'Maria Lisa.'

She watched the door close behind him, and the breath left her body in a shaking sob.

Yes, she thought, tomorrow would indeed be different...

Amalfi looked even more beautiful with the approach of autumn, although Marisa still wasn't sure why she'd decided to return there, when the obvious course had been to fly straight back to England. After all, she was co-owner of a gallery in London, so there was work waiting for her. And everyone said that work was a solace—didn't they? So if she worked hard enough and long enough the pain might begin to subside.

Except that she wasn't working. She was sitting

under a lemon tree in a garden, looking at the sea. The wheel had turned full circle, and she was back at the beginning, more alone than ever.

Leaving the Clinica had been much easier than she'd expected. After all, she'd hardly been a patient needing medical sanction to be discharged. So she had simply woken after a sedative-induced night's sleep, dressed and walked out, moving confidently, her head high. Bearing, she'd hoped, no resemblance to the broken, weeping girl of yesterday.

She'd taken a taxi to the Villa Proserpina—a quick phone call having ascertained that Signor Lorenzo had left very early that morning to visit his father the Marchese in Milano, and that therefore the coast was clear.

No one at the house had seemed anxious about her absence, probably because they thought she'd decided to follow Renzo to Zurich after all.

Once in their suite it had been the work of minutes to pack a bag and retrieve her passport. And a second's pause to leave the letter she had struggled to write the previous evening on the mantelpiece in the *salotto* for Renzo to find on his return.

She had kept it brief, stating only that it was impossible, under the changed circumstances, for their marriage to continue, and that she would sign whatever was necessary to obtain their mutual freedom as soon as her lawyers received the papers. Adding that she wished him well.

Then she'd gone downstairs, walked out into the sunshine, got into her car and driven away.

It was better this way. Better to take the initiative, as she kept telling herself, even though leaving like that, without a proper word to anyone, like a thief in the night, had torn her apart. But it had been infinitely preferable to the anguish of an interview with Renzo—hearing from his own lips that her brief shining happiness had to end.

And Signora Barzati had said he would be generous, therefore he would hardly begrudge her the car he'd given her, or the money she would need to spend in order to remove herself from his life.

Not that she'd spent that much. Just petrol, her meals, and payment for the past three nights in a simple room above the *trattoria* in the village. No five-star luxury for this trip, she thought. Not that it had ever mattered to her. For her, the greatest luxury of all had always been the man she loved, lying beside her in the night.

But she wouldn't be staying long in this place where she'd once found a kind of peace, because, to her astonishment, the Casa Adriana had been sold.

She'd learned this from Mrs Morton, who was still fighting the good fight in the garden, even though her days there were numbered, because, as she said, the new owners were bound to have their own outside staff.

'The builders move in next week,' she'd told Marisa. 'I'm almost sorry, although it's good that such a lovely place will realise its full potential at last.' She smiled. 'Someone else must have fallen in love with the view, my dear.'

Marisa made herself smile back. 'Well, I hope Adriana approves of them, that's all.'

'Ah,' Mrs Morton said softly. 'So it was that old story that drew you back?' She paused. 'Will you tell me something, my dear? Because I've often wondered. When you were here before, there was a young man who used to come and stand at the gate each day and watch you. Tall and very attractive. Did you ever meet him?'

The breath caught in Marisa's throat. 'Someone at the gate?' she managed. 'I never knew...'

'He would never come in,' said Mrs Morton. 'Which made me sorry, because it seemed to me that he was just as sad as you were alone, and I hoped that somehow you might find each other.'

Hurt, Marisa thought, *and lonely*. Ottavia had apparently been right. She looked at the kind face and forced a smile. 'We did—for a while,' she said. 'But it didn't last.'

'Because you were already married, perhaps? I don't judge, my dear, but I can't help notice you're wearing a ring now.'

'Yes,' Marisa said quietly. 'Exactly because I was...married.'

Mrs Morton had completed her tasks and left, returning to her apartment, her husband, the waiting drink on the terrace and the comfortable discussion of the day's events. Her marriage, in fact.

And I should leave too, Marisa thought, sighing. *In fact, I should never have come back to this place, with all its resonances. Because there's no comfort or peace here for me any more, and I was a fool to expect it.*

I don't have faith and hope to sustain me, as Adriana did, and I can't sit here, letting my life drift by, eternally waiting for something that reality and my own common sense tells me will never happen.

She thought again of what Mrs Morton had said. That Renzo—*Renzo*—had followed her here each day and never said anything—then or later...

If I'd only known, she thought, and stopped with a little gasp. Because, she realised suddenly, she had known. She'd been aware, so many times, of something—some presence—that had made her feel less lonely but which she'd dismissed, telling herself that she was simply letting Adriana's legend get to her rather too much.

She lifted her head and stared at the restless sea, her eyes stinging with the tears she'd refused to let herself shed since she'd left Tuscany.

Oh, darling, she whispered silently. *Why didn't you come in? Why didn't you walk down the garden and sit beside me?*

Not that it would have made any real difference, she reminded herself in anguish. Their story would still be ending, like that of Adriana and Filippo, in separation and loss. But at least they would have had all those other wasted months together. Another store of memories for her to draw on in the utter blankness ahead.

'Maria Lisa.' She might have imagined his voice, born out of her own desperate yearning, but not the hand on her shoulder.

'Renzo!' She turned to face him, acutely aware of the blurred eyes and trembling mouth she hadn't allowed him to see at their last meeting. 'What are you doing here?'

'Following my wife,' he said. He came round the bench and sat beside her. 'And I would have been here much sooner if I had not seen your passport was gone and wasted time looking for you in England.' The dark, haggard face tried to smile. 'Your business partner now thinks I am insane, bursting in on him like a wild man and demanding you back.'

He paused. 'And then I remembered this place, and I wondered.'

'Oh, God,' she said hoarsely. 'Couldn't you have shown a little mercy and just—let me go?'

'Never,' he said. 'Not while I have life. How could you not know that?'

'But I can't be your wife. Not any longer,' she whispered. 'For your family's sake you have to have an heir, and I can't have children. You know that. So you have to find someone else to marry, who won't fail you. Someone you can love—' She broke off, swallowing. 'And I can't— I won't stand in your way.'

'But you do stand in the way, Maria Lisa,' he said gently. 'And you always will, *mi amore*. Because all the love that I have is for you. I see no one else, hear no other voice, want only you.'

His shaking hands framed her face as he kissed her wet eyes, her cheeks and parted, unhappy lips.

'Believe me,' he whispered between kisses. 'My love, my sweet one, believe me, and come back to me.'

'But when you came to see me in hospital,' she said huskily, 'you were so cold—like a stranger.'

'They told me that you were heartbroken,' he said. 'That it had been impossible to calm you. Therefore it was impressed upon me that I could not give way. That, as your husband, I had to be strong for us both or your emotional recovery might be impeded. So I dared not come near you. Dared not touch you or kiss you, *carissima*, or I too would have been lost. Because I knew that all I wanted was to lie beside you, put my head on your breasts and weep. I told myself—tomorrow will be different. Tomorrow we can find comfort in our love for each other.' He gave a shuddering sigh. 'And then I came back from Zurich with Papa and you were gone, leaving just that little note. And then I did weep, Maria Lisa, sitting alone in the room we'd shared. Because I thought that maybe I was wrong, and that you had not begun to love me during these last happy weeks together. That, after all, your independence mattered more to you than I did.'

He shook his head. 'But I also remembered all your warmth and sweetness—how Zurich had been hell without you. And I told myself that I would get you back, no matter how long it took or whatever obstacles were in the way.'

She touched his cheek with hesitant fingertips. 'I was so unhappy I just wanted to die,' she said. 'But it makes no difference.' She paused. 'Darling, your grandmother came to see me, and even though I hated everything she said I knew she was right. That if I loved you I would have to give you up.'

'She telephoned me,' he said grimly. 'Telling me that she grieved for me but hoped, once you had gone, I would be sensible and do my duty.'

'But don't you see?' she said in a low voice. 'If you hadn't wanted a child you wouldn't have married me or anyone else.'

'That may have been true once,' Renzo admitted wryly. 'But when you came to stand beside me in church, and I put my ring on your finger, I knew I would not have changed places with anyone on earth. And that somehow I had to persuade you to feel the same.' He shook his head. 'But that was my failure, and I can never forgive myself for it, or for what followed. Those weeks of our honeymoon were a living nightmare, *carissima*. I wanted so badly to put things right between us, but I did not know how to begin.'

'Was that why you used to follow me, but never let me know?'

'I needed to find out what drew you here every day,' Renzo said simply. 'And as you seemed contented I could not intrude and spoil it for you.'

'But if you felt like that,' she said shakily, 'why—why did you send me away?'

He said roughly, 'Because I heard you crying and I thought you could not face the prospect of having to live with me as my wife. That I had scared and disgusted you too much.'

'No,' she said softly. 'I was crying because I knew I'd really wanted our baby so that there would be someone in my life I could love without reservation.'

'And I wanted you to love me,' he said. 'To give me another chance to make you happy. That was what I tried to say in all those letters you did not read.'

He slipped off the bench and knelt beside her, his head in her lap.

'So will you take me now, Maria Lisa?' he asked, his voice uneven. 'Will you believe that our marriage means more to me than anything in the world, and love me as I love you, *mi adorata*, and even after this sadness live with me, let us build our future together?'

'Yes,' she said, stroking his hair. 'Oh, my dearest love, yes.'

Perhaps Adriana was right, she thought, as later they walked from the garden, hand in hand, knowing they would never come back there. That they had all they needed.

Perhaps faith and hope would always prevail. And then healing could begin.

Or that was what she would believe.

And Maria Lisa Santangeli smiled up at her husband.

MILLS & BOON PUBLISH EIGHT LARGE PRINT TITLES A MONTH. THESE ARE THE EIGHT TITLES FOR MAY 2009.

———————— ෙ ————————

THE BILLIONAIRE'S BRIDE OF VENGEANCE
Miranda Lee

THE SANTANGELI MARRIAGE
Sara Craven

THE SPANIARD'S VIRGIN HOUSEKEEPER
Diana Hamilton

THE GREEK TYCOON'S RELUCTANT BRIDE
Kate Hewitt

NANNY TO THE BILLIONAIRE'S SON
Barbara McMahon

CINDERELLA AND THE SHEIKH
Natasha Oakley

PROMOTED: SECRETARY TO BRIDE!
Jennie Adams

THE BLACK SHEEP'S PROPOSAL
Patricia Thayer

MILLS & BOON®
Pure reading pleasure™

0509 Rom LP

MILLS & BOON PUBLISH EIGHT LARGE PRINT TITLES A MONTH. THESE ARE THE EIGHT TITLES FOR JUNE 2009.

CR

THE RUTHLESS MAGNATE'S VIRGIN MISTRESS
Lynne Graham

THE GREEK'S FORCED BRIDE
Michelle Reid

THE SHEIKH'S REBELLIOUS MISTRESS
Sandra Marton

THE PRINCE'S WAITRESS WIFE
Sarah Morgan

THE AUSTRALIAN'S SOCIETY BRIDE
Margaret Way

THE ROYAL MARRIAGE ARRANGEMENT
Rebecca Winters

TWO LITTLE MIRACLES
Caroline Anderson

MANHATTAN BOSS, DIAMOND PROPOSAL
Trish Wylie

MILLS & BOON
Pure reading pleasure